Saving SCOTTY

Garry Braun

Cover Art by Larissa Raine

ISBN: 978-1-4866-2667-0
eBook ISBN: 978-1-4866-2668-7

Word Alive Press
119 De Baets Street Winnipeg, MB R2J 3R9
www.wordalivepress.ca

WORD ALIVE
—P R E S S—

Cataloguing in Publication information can be obtained from Library and Archives Canada.

This book is dedicated to my children, Luke, Larissa, and Joel.
You grew up in Mali, West Africa playing with a dog
who bears a striking resemblance to one in this story.

Acknowledgements

This book would not have been possible without the encouragement of my wife. Thank you, Rita Mae, for believing in me.

I also want to thank Wendy Sawatzky, who gave excellent feedback on my very rough first draft.

Rachael Adcock, I'm grateful for your timely advice and counsel along the journey.

Thank you to Larissa Raine, who so marvellously crafted the front cover of this book.

Thank you to all the kind people at Word Alive Press who helped to see this project through to its conclusion.

I'm forever grateful for the many friends, colleagues, and dogs I was privileged to know in Mali, West Africa.

Most of all, thanks be to God who designed us to be creative.

Prologue

The year is 2019. West African countries are generally stable, although travel precautions are in place for politically volatile areas. Non-government agencies from the United States and Canada work actively alongside national partners, promoting small-scale cottage industries in Burkina Faso and Mali. It's a time of great optimism, but there is also unease on the streets of Ouagadougou as rumours of insurgent activity circulate with increasing frequency.

Kyla, along with her furry traveling companion, Scotty, is heading to this city. She works for an NGO in Canada focused on promoting small business in West Africa. At the last minute, she asked her boss about taking her dog along. To Kyla's surprise and delight, he agreed.

SCOTTY

Short breaths, I told myself, shivering in the frigid air. This wasn't like a winter walk in Saskatchewan. This was the kind of cold that invites itself in and makes its bed on your favourite blanket. Even worse, tantalizing smells were driving me mad with desire... but as long as I was stuck in my kennel, they remained frustratingly inaccessible. The scents of dried cereal, chocolate, chewable candy, and dried fruit teased me. It reminded me of the farmers' market in Regina.

But I definitely was *not* in a farmers' market now.

A low rumbling sent vibrations through the floor of my kennel and I began to wonder whether I would ever live to smell anything again.

But wait, I haven't even introduced myself. My name is Scotty, and I'm a Scottish terrier-schnauzer mix. You must think my owner quite unoriginal to have named me Scotty, but I've never held that against her.

I don't remember my first days as a puppy. I don't remember being adopted by my human parent in Regina, Saskatchewan. Frankly, if any dog tells you they remember those kinds of details, you have the right to remain dubious.

1

My memory kicks in the day I was given credit for saving the life of an infant.

I was out for a walk in Wascana Park, a lovely green space in the heart of the city. Our walk came to a standstill when Kyla—that's my owner—stopped to talk to a friend. It was a windy day, and as the two of them chatted I noticed an unattended stroller begin to move. Kyla and her friend were so engrossed in their conversation that neither saw it roll away.

I yelped and pulled frantically on my leash.

They both looked up to see the stroller gathering speed toward the lake. Kyla was quickest. She barrelled down the path and caught the handle of the stroller mere feet from the edge of the water.

The mother of the child came running to the scene, a toddler in her arms. Turns out she had been chasing her toddler in the grass when the stroller began to roll. I could tell by her tears and demeanour that she was visibly upset.

Suddenly everyone was looking my way, pointing at me, lifting me up, and hugging and kissing me. Frankly, it was a bit much. I was just doing what dogs do.

Unlike that exciting first memory, the rest of my puppyhood memories were normal. Regina was a good place to grow up and I was a whiz at house-training. One quick bark at the door and Kyla would let me out to do my business.

One thing I'll say about Kyla is that she never left me outside for long on those minus-forty-degree days when all I wanted was to get back into the house and plant myself next to the heating register in the kitchen. The linoleum felt so wondrously warm after those cold excursions to the back yard.

Kyla was a stickler for walks even on brisk days, but she never dragged me out when it was bitterly cold, and I loved her for that.

But on one blustery day, I noticed that Kyla seemed to be preoccupied with preparations of some kind. She was filling suitcases with clothes that didn't seem to be at all appropriate for Canadian winters. Sundresses, hats, sandals… all the things you'd associate with summer. I found this confusing. From past experience, I knew that summer couldn't possibly have arrived yet.

My answer came a few days later when Kyla coaxed me into my kennel, put a warm blanket overtop, and carried me out to a waiting car. She left me momentarily in the back seat before returning with those suitcases I had seen her packing. She climbed in beside me, flipped off the blanket still covering my kennel, and said something to the man in the front seat. We were soon moving down the road.

When it's just Kyla and me, she usually opens the passenger side window and I stick my nose out to sniff the air. I love sniffing the air when I'm in her car. It feels like I'm getting supercharged air into my lungs as we hurtle down the road.

Stuck in my kennel this time, though, I whined. Kyla must have understood because she spoke some soothing words that instantly made me feel better. If she wasn't nervous or upset, I decided that I wouldn't be either.

We got to a place where there were lots of other cars just like the one we were in. People were grabbing suitcases and loading them onto carts. Then they were pushing these carts through a door that led inside a big building.

Kyla let me stay in the car while she loaded her suitcases. She then perched my kennel on top of all the bags.

Pretty soon we were inside. I had never seen a building this big! People seemed to be rushing everywhere, making their way to a counter with official-looking ladies in blue uniforms behind it. It seemed like these ladies were the bosses. They looked at papers, hit their fingers on a machine, and then put the bags on a moving sidewalk.

The first lady in blue smiled when she saw me riding atop all the bags. She said something to Kyla and then made all those gushy sounds people make when they talk to dogs. I don't know why people change their voices when they talk to dogs. It's always puzzled me, but I've learned that they mean no disrespect.

Kyla handed over her papers, which the lady studied before tapping her fingers on her machine. The two bags soon disappeared behind a curtain and I was relieved to find that I wasn't being sent along with them! No, Kyla picked me up and walked over to another line. Here she had to take off her belt, surrender her purse, put her keys in a tray, and walk through a tent. My kennel went through a dark tunnel and I emerged to see Kyla waiting for me.

She got dressed again, picked up her things, and carried me over to a place where many people were sitting in rows of chairs. She fished out my leash, clipped it onto my collar, and let me out of my kennel. It was the first time I had been able to stretch my legs since we'd left home and it felt good.

She waited until no one was in the washroom, then took me inside and laid down a wad of paper towels on the floor. She

4

pointed and I didn't have to be asked twice. I emptied my bladder on the towels, stepped aside, and let Kyla throw them in the garbage.

I love her. She always seems to know exactly what I need.

Once I was back in my kennel, a man came to take me away. Kyla waved goodbye to me and didn't seem to be concerned. The man took me to a dark room and placed me inside a large area with lots of suitcases and bags. Although my eyes eventually adjusted, I remained confused. The food scents and biting cold weren't like anything I'd ever experienced. Wherever this was, I didn't like the idea of being separated from Kyla.

A low, steady droning sound, coupled with stress-induced fatigue, put me into a deep sleep. In what seemed like only two shakes of my tail, I heard something that sounded like the flushing of the world's biggest toilet. My kennel bounced a little, and then the sensation of movement finally ceased.

When the room went all quiet, a big door opened and light came flooding in. It was bright and the air was hot. A man took my kennel and put it onto a platform with lots of bags and suitcases.

Peanut butter smells wafted out from the bag in front of me, reminding me that I hadn't eaten for a long time.

As the platform started moving, I began to wonder where Kyla was. I was placed on another one of those moving sidewalks. Everything in me wanted to bark, but something told me that it wouldn't be wise.

Before long I was lifted down and set beside some boxes and crates. I couldn't see other dogs anywhere and my fright intensified. I began to worry that Kyla wouldn't come to fetch me.

After an eternity in that hot, stuffy room, I began to wonder if this was to be my permanent home.

Finally, a group of men in army fatigues and black polished boots entered. I decided to make my presence known, and it seemed as if the men were startled by my barking.

I saw them talk and point at me. Then one of them came to my kennel and picked it up. I really didn't care where we were going; I just wanted to get out of that stuffy room.

Soon I was brought outside to a water spigot with a short garden hose attached. The man who had carried me set my kennel down, opened the spigot, and let some water trickle into my enclosure. I've never been so glad to drink some water! I lapped it up like it was going to be my last drink. The water was warm, but I didn't care. My spirits revived as soon as my tongue tasted the life-giving liquid.

The man in fatigues motioned with his hand and soon a green car pulled up next to my kennel. I was loaded onto the floor through the rear passenger side door. I was too tired and confused to bark. My strategy now was to make as little commotion as possible and hope the car would take me to Kyla.

I don't know how it happened, but I fell asleep. I was vaguely aware of some people in the back seat, but the combination of the hum of the wheels and the forward motion had its effect.

I awoke just as the car came to a stop. The door opened and a man roughly grabbed the handle of my kennel and hoisted me up and out of the car.

Kyla

Kyla Bouvier settled back into her seat, fidgeting with her cushion. She wedged it between her seatback and the window, closed her eyes, and imagined how good it would feel to stretch her legs again. She was flying economy, but at least she was next to the window.

Earlier she had marvelled at the vastness of the Sahara desert. Its undulating sands had seemed to stretch on forever. Now, sitting on the tarmac at Bamako International Airport, waiting for the plane to refuel, she remembered that in less than two hours she would be in Ouagadougou, reunited once more with her little Scotty. Would he be all right? The travel agent had assured her that pets were well taken care of.

From the skies, Ouagadougou didn't seem dissimilar to Bamako. Night had fallen and the lights were clearly visible long before the plane began its descent. Kyla involuntarily gripped the armrest. She could live without the hitch in her stomach that always accompanied landings. The risks seemed to increase in her mind as she pondered all that could possibly go wrong. Not that she had the faintest idea of what was involved in landing a huge 707, but she never breathed easily until the plane had come to a complete stop on the tarmac.

The landing was smooth.

Her legs were tired, but she felt more alive as she approached arrivals. She fished out her international health card and passport from her backpack and presented them to the guard at the gate. He waved her through without comment and she followed the other passengers to the baggage carousel. Like crows descending on fresh roadkill, Burkinabe boys aggressively jockeyed for position at her side.

"Madame, laissez-moi porter votre baggage," they each said.

"Non, c'est moi!" a particularly tall boy exclaimed as he pushed one of the smaller boys aside.

Having been warned about this, Kyla laid her hand on the shoulders of one of the less intrusive boys.

"Toi," she said. "Tu veux porter mes effets?"

"Oui," he replied. "Avec plaisir."

Seeing that one of them had been selected to take care of her bags, the other boys scattered to offer their services to other disembarking passengers.

Kyla indicated a suitcase that was maroon in colour and her porter reached out to grab it. He had already procured a luggage cart.

"Are there others?" he asked.

"Yes, there should be two more."

The rest of the bags were soon stacked on the luggage cart.

"Allez-y, madame." In passable English, he added, "Follow me."

"Not yet. I'm waiting for my pet dog."

"Pet dog?" The boy's face was the picture of confusion.

"Yes, do you know where the dogs are offloaded?"

It was never good form to appear to be at a loss, so the young man simply said, "Wait here. I'll be right back."

He returned with a man in military uniform. Kyla had seen pictures of Thomas Sankara, the former president of Burkina Faso who had been killed in 1987. The man who stood before her bore a striking resemblance to Sankara.

"Madame, je peux vous aider?" he asked.

"She speaks English," the porter interposed.

The army man seemed to relax. Kyla was aware of strong anti-French sentiment in the country and she rightly assumed that an American—or in her case, Canadian—might be treated with more respect and friendliness than a French woman.

"What can I do for you, ma'am?" he said.

"Well, if you can direct me to the area where they offload pets, I need to pick up my dog."

Kyla could tell by the expression on the man's face that he wasn't entirely sure of what he was being asked.

"Well," came the delayed response. "I'll have to ask my superior. Just wait here if you will."

Kyla nodded. Where else would she go at this point?

A picture of military efficiency, the young man moved through a throng of passengers toward a glassed-in area to her right. The man disappeared into the office.

Several minutes later, he returned.

"My boss says he knows what you're talking about, but there were no pets on this flight. He double-checked with both

9

the supervisor of luggage and the head of customs. No one was aware of a pet of any kind being offloaded."

Kyla struggled to keep her composure. Feeling herself unravel, she reached for her phone. A picture of Scotty occupied the screen.

"Here," Kyla said. "This is what he looks like. Please help me find him."

To his credit, the military man didn't dismiss her plea. "Look, let's go ask my boss again. Maybe there's been some kind of error."

A few minutes later she was watching as the man explained the situation to a middle-aged man sitting behind a desk with a keyboard and computer screen off to one side. The man behind the desk alternately stared at the screen and typed in flight information.

"This may take a minute," he said.

Kyla was losing patience. "Scotty has to be somewhere! I know for a fact that he was loaded onto the plane in Paris!"

"You're right. It's showing that he was loaded onto your flight."

"Oh, thank God. That means he must be somewhere in the airport."

"Not necessarily, ma'am."

"What do you mean, 'not necessarily'?"

"You landed in Bamako, correct?"

"Yes."

"And you didn't get off the plane there?"

"No, I didn't. They said anyone continuing on to Ouagaduodou must stay on the plane. Why are you asking all these questions about Bamako?"

"Ma'am, I've known my luggage supervisor for twenty years. He's extremely thorough. If he says there was no dog offloaded on this flight, we have to consider the possibility that your dog was accidentally offloaded in Bamako."

Kyla's shoulders slumped in despair. In a language she had never heard before, the supervisor behind the desk gave a command and the man in military fatigues left brusquely.

He returned with a bottle of water, which he handed to Kyla. She was touched by this gesture. She felt like screaming, but she had already decided that losing her mind would be unproductive. The cool water on her parched throat helped clear her mind.

"So what can be done to get him back?" she asked finally.

"Unfortunately, there isn't another flight from Bamako to Ouagadougou until Thursday. I'll contact my counterpart in Bamako and we'll try to get your pet on that flight. In the meantime, I'm sure he'll be well taken care of."

"I'd like you to phone your counterpart right now, if you could, please."

"I'm afraid that won't be possible."

"And why not?" Kyla's voice betrayed her frustration.

"Because, ma'am, it's coming up to midnight and my colleagues will have left the airport by now."

"Surely there's a mobile phone number where he could be reached."

"I'm afraid not, ma'am."

"Look, Mr. …" Here she paused to allow him to fill in the name.

"Coulibaly. And your name, ma'am?"

"Bouvier. Mr. Coulibaly, as you may appreciate, my pet is special to me. I was hesitant to make this trip because I don't enjoy traveling. Having my dog with me was a concession my boss afforded me to make the trip more pleasant. I'm here representing a firm that invests plenty of money into your great country. I am certain that losing a pet in transit isn't something you would want added to your file."

Coulibaly was already dialling a number. He put the phone on speaker mode so Kyla could hear the ringtone.

The number rang a dozen times with no one picking up.

The supervisor hung up the phone and looked across the desk at Madame Bouvier.

"Madame, I assure you that I will be in contact with my counterpart in Bamako at first light and we will get to the bottom of this. How can we contact you?"

Kyla reached into her backpack and pulled out a business card. "I will await your call tomorrow morning, Mr. Coulibaly. I'm sorry if I came across as abrupt, but you can appreciate the gravity of my situation, I'm sure."

"Absolutely!" Coulibaly replied. "I will have my counterpart in Bamako call you the minute I have any news. His name is Mungolo Traoré."

"Thank you." And with that, she gathered up her backpack, wallet, and phone. "Goodbye, Mr. Coulibaly."

SCOTTY

I had no idea how long we'd been on the road, but my kennel was soon lifted out of the car. I willed my eyes to come to life, but it was the dead of night—of that, I was certain—and this was unlike any place I'd ever seen before. I could hear animals. I heard a donkey braying, other dogs barking, and men visiting.

Peering out from behind the wire mesh of my kennel, I also saw a small fire and the smell of tea wafting out from a small teapot on hot coals. Kyla used to take me outside overnight, so the scene of people sitting around a fire was familiar.

My kennel was set down on the ground while the men conferred, pointing toward me occasionally. One squatted down beside my kennel and held a bone in front of me. I'm ashamed to admit this, because Kyla had drilled it into me not to accept food from strangers, but as hungry as I was I pulled the chicken bone through the wire mesh and gnawed at it like it was going to be my last meal. The man laughed at this, but I really didn't care.

He then opened my kennel and tied my leash around a nearby tree as I continued to have my way with the bone. He soon placed a tin plate of water in front of me so I could satisfy my thirst.

Apparently I was the evening's entertainment. Fifteen or twenty kids were staring at me, pointing, giggling, and daring one another to get close. Eventually the adults came to collect the children and I was led inside a small enclosure. I still wore my leash, but that was the least of my worries. Once inside the enclosure, I heard a metal door clank close behind me and a key turn in the lock. I whimpered and barked for several minutes, but no one came.

When I heard a voice yell in my direction, I recognized its tone—displeasure and threat all wrapped up in one.

What was happening to me? Where was I? More importantly, where was Kyla?

I took stock of the room. Huge bags were stacked to the ceiling. A mouse scurried across the mud floor and into a tiny hole in the corner. I was in a storeroom of some kind. The bags gave off a grainy odour not unlike a smell I had once encountered back in Saskatchewan when Kyla took me on a trip to visit her cousin's farm.

I noticed a slight crack in the floor against one of the walls and took a few tentative scratches at the gap. With a little effort, I realized I might be able to dig my way out. Digging had never been a problem for me. I love digging. When I was a pup, Kyla would get exasperated by how many times I dug my way under the backyard fence and into the back alley.

Within minutes, I had created a sizable hole under the wall. Just a bit more and I'd be out.

And that's exactly what happened. I dug my way out and was soon sniffing the open night air.

Intuitively I knew that the less noise I made, the better. I just wanted to get back to Kyla, but where was she? I ran down the dirt road. Despite my best efforts to avoid drawing attention, the night air was soon filled with barking. I heard human voices too. They sounded a lot like the voices I'd heard back in Regina when owners wanted their dogs to quiet down.

I ran as fast as my little legs could carry me—directionless, but fast.

That's when it happened. A brown mutt was suddenly trotting along beside me, nipping at my ear to get my attention. I slowed to a trot and eventually stopped altogether so I could communicate better with this four-leg.

Before he said anything, he sniffed my nose and circled around to my butt. I returned the favour. To humans this must seem mysterious, but trust me, I can tell a lot from the scents I pick up when I take a few moments to sniff.

My new acquaintance yelped a greeting. "Hey little guy, who are you and how did you get here?"

"I wish I knew. The how-did-I-get-here part, I mean. My name is Scotty."

"Pleased to meet you, Scotty. Name's Police. You were just digging, weren't you? Smells like Samake's yard."

"Yes, I was just digging. I was thrown into a little room and left there. When I saw the beginnings of a hole in the floor, I dug my way out. And here I am."

Police seemed friendly enough, but I needed to be moving on. I broke into a trot heading in the same direction as before.

Police scampered up alongside. "Listen, little buddy—"

"Scotty," I corrected. I'd never liked being called *little* and regardless of cultural customs I expected Police could afford me at least this much respect.

"Okay, Scotty, you can't just run off into the night like a crazy dog. You need to make a plan. I don't know where you come from, but you look pretty normal to me, apart from the fact that your hair is a mess and your legs look like little sausages on a grill. Where exactly are you gettin' to?"

"Away from here, okay? I just want to get back to where Kyla is."

By now, I was beginning to see Police's point. Running aimlessly wasn't going to help me find Kyla any quicker.

I stopped. I needed water.

"Any water in this town?" I asked.

"Yeah. Just follow me."

Police brought me to a metal spigot protruding from a rectangular piece of metal inset in concrete. There were puddles everywhere and I drank until my thirst was quenched. The water was cool and satisfying.

"What is this place?" I asked.

"They call this a pump. You've never seen one before?"

"No."

"Wow, my friend. You are a strange little guy. I've never met a dog who hasn't seen a pump before. Folks come here and move that handle up and down. Before long, water comes gushing out. How do dog-folks get their water where you're from?"

"There's this wee little miniature handle inside the house. My human just turns it and water comes out. Then she puts my dish underneath and I get my water."

"Crazy! So… what's your plan?"

"Listen. When I dug myself out of the mud room just now, I really didn't have much of a plan. I just wanna find my owner."

"Okay," said Police. "Let's think about this. When was the last time you saw this lady you call Kyla?"

"I don't know. A long time ago. Honestly, Police, these last few days have been a nightmare. My kennel was put into a container. It was cold and I heard a constant roar that hurt my ears. Now I'm here. It just doesn't make any sense."

By now a crowd of dogs had gathered by the pump and it seemed wise to move on. Police and I walked toward the shade of a nearby tree.

"What's up with little stinky breath there, Police?" one of the leaner mutts barked.

"Hey, I can understand everything you're saying," I called back. "I may be little, but my ears work fine. And I dare say my breath is a tad bit fresher than yours, mate."

The remark was met with a look of incredulity from Exposed Ribcage. I wondered when he had enjoyed his last square meal.

Now that I looked around at the other dogs, Police seemed to be one of the few who was decently full.

"All right, listen up everydog," Police said. "Scotty here dropped in on us from who knows where, but we've gotta think about what our next move is before it gets light out. Who's got an idea?"

Before anydog had a chance to answer, a shrill whistle pierced the air.

"That's for me," announced a black and brown dog with a short, stubby tail. "I gotta peace out. If I don't get back quick, I'll be on the rope again. Let me know what you decide. I'd say hightailing it to the next village, rising sun direction, might be his only safe bet. But what do I know?"

"See ya, Nicky," Police said. "You might have something there. We'll let you know what happens." After Nicky had run off, Police turned back to me. "I don't like the thought of just running without a plan. It seems desperate and impulsive."

"Agreed," I said. "But desperate is how I'm feeling right now."

"Let's think about this for a minute." Police sat his butt down. "The people who put you in the mud room, how did they seem to you?"

"I'm not sure I follow you."

"Well, for example, were they rough with you? Did they hit you, kick you, that sort of thing?"

"No, they just left me in the room and closed the door. I wouldn't say they were overly kind, but they did feed me and give me some water."

"Hmm. Something tells me that running isn't going to work out in your favour, Scotty."

"So what do we do?"

"Come on. Follow me. I have an idea."

It's funny. With some dogs, you just know you're going to be friends. That's how it was with Police. There didn't seem to be a malicious bone in his body.

So when Police rose from his haunches and started trotting away, I didn't hesitate. I just followed him.

"Where are we going?" I asked.

"You'll see."

We weaved in and out of pathways surrounded by mud walls, like running through a maze. We hadn't gone that far when I realized I would never be able to retrace my steps. I just ran fast enough to keep Police's tail in sight. All the while, my nostrils inhaled strong scents. Kyla used to spread lotion on her feet and ankles in winter. Multiply that smell by one hundred and you'd have some idea of what I was dealing with.

We rounded one more corner, burst through an opening in the mud wall, and came to a halt in an enclosed yard.

"Here we are. We'll be safe here, I promise." Police lay down under a tree and I did the same.

"So if you don't mind me asking, where are we?" I asked.

"This, my little furry friend, is where I live. They feed me well, they expect me to bark when strangers come around, and they don't throw things at me, which is more than I can say for most of my friends. I have some good two-legs here."

"It's still dark, but it won't be long before your two-legs, as you call them, are going to wake up. What are they going to do when they see a misfit like me hanging out with you?"

"Oh, don't you worry about that, little buddy. Nobody's going to harm you on my watch."

We sat still for a few minutes, listening to the night sounds. A donkey brayed loudly, the last few hiccoughs trailing off like a symphonic decrescendo. An early rooster heralded the dawn.

"Police?"

"Yeah?"

"Why are you doing this?"

"Doing what?"

"Why are you being so kind to me?"

"Ah, don't get all mushy on me, buddy. I know a good dog when I see one. You're a good one, Scotty. I couldn't just leave you all alone. Anydog would have done the same thing."

"I'm not so sure. I've seen some mean ones in my day. Anyway, thanks."

"No problem. Now close those eyes and catch a few winks, Scotty. It's going to be a busy day."

He didn't have to ask twice, because I was soon drifting off. The trauma and tiredness saw to that.

Kyla

Kyla managed to wrest a few hours of rest from what otherwise would have been a sleepless night. She just couldn't believe the ineptitude of a transport system that had dropped the ball so thoroughly. She didn't even know who to blame. In the meantime, and this was the biggest hole in her heart, she felt somehow that this was all her fault. What had she been thinking bringing a dog on a trip to West Africa, a place she knew from experience to have unique and maddening challenges?

She swung her feet onto the tile floor of her hotel room and considered her next move. She didn't hold out much hope of receiving news about her little Scotty.

The warm shower awakened her senses, and as she got dressed she thought about where she could get some decent coffee. She regarded herself in the small wall mirror beside the door and had to smile in spite of her circumstances. With her tan skirt, beige blouse, and sunglasses, she looked like she would fit in on the streets of L.A.

Phone in hand, she closed and locked the hotel room door and turned to face a cacophony of car horns, taximen yelling their destinations, and vendors carrying everything from earthen pots to bolts of fabric atop their heads. Yes, she was in Burkina Faso.

More importantly, she could smell coffee. A quick glance down the street revealed a long wooden table in front of a brick wall, a blue plastic tablecloth stretched across it. A crude bench supported several patrons sipping hot beverages from large plastic cups. Small tins of coffee and powdered milk were displayed on a makeshift wooden shelf affixed to a cement wall. A hand-painted sign read "Touré Cafe."

"Good morning, Madame. How are you this fine new day?" asked the proprietor, a little too cheerily for Kyla's liking.

"Fine, thank you. And how are you?"

"No troubles, none whatsoever. And what can I serve you this morning?"

By now Kyla's senses had fully awakened and the baguettes peeking out from their plastic wrapping papers called to her. Fresh jam completed the picture.

"I'll have a coffee with a slice of bread please."

"Right away, madame. Or is it mademoiselle?"

Kyla nearly winced at the formal reminder that she was still single. "You can just call me Kyla," she said, avoiding the question.

"And you have the pleasure of being served today by Abdul," the man replied with a smile, busying himself with the task of ladling out some steaming hot water from the cauldron behind him.

"Nice to meet you, Abdul."

Kyla glanced at an abandoned newspaper beside her. It must have been a small-town publication because, to her surprise, the conference she was participating in had a headline near the bottom of the first page: *Ouagadougou to Host Micro-Enterprise Conference.*

Abdul placed the steaming hot plastic mug in front of Kyla atop the kitschy plastic tablecloth. Pulling a hand cloth from his apron, he dispatched some breadcrumbs to the earth behind him.

Kyla knew the drill. Her parents had been missionaries in Mali, a neighbouring country to the west. As a girl, she remembered walking with her dad through markets and along streets just like the one she was on now. She picked up a spoon, dug into the nearest tin, and transferred two heaping scoops of coffee into her mug, gently stirring. Next she reached for a tin of sweetened condensed milk and poured a generous amount into her mug.

Her first sip was glorious. For a brief moment, she forgot that she was in a foreign country waiting for a conference to begin while worrying over what had happened to her Scotty.

Abdul placed half a baguette in front of her, taking care to slide a plastic knife, spoon, and jar of strawberry jam in her direction.

"Thank you, Abdul. You are too kind."

"Not at all, Kyla. Enjoy!" Abdul turned to fill a waiting customer's mug with hot water.

The baguette wasn't unlike the bread she remembered wolfing down as a little girl. It was funny how tastes and smells could take her back to childhood so effectively. If only she could find bread this tasty in Regina…

Kyla scanned her phone messages to see whether anything had come from Coulibaly in Bamako. She doubted there would be any news. And given how she had left things, she was sure any news would come by phone call, not text.

Taking a last swig of coffee, Kyla reached into her wallet and pulled out 250 francs. According to the list pegged onto the brick wall, the price for her breakfast was only 200 francs, but she wanted to leave a bit of a tip for the kind proprietor.

"Thank you, Kyla. You are very generous. I hope to see you again tomorrow?"

"You well might, Abdul. Have a good day."

"You as well." He held his hand to his heart in the West African way.

Kyla knew the way to the conference. She decided to head to the corner of Independence Drive and Rue Verre. Not one to leave anything to chance, she had researched the neighbourhood even before leaving Regina.

She joined the army of pedestrians. Forgetting her white skin, she walked with purpose, like she remembered her father doing. "The last thing you want to do in West Africa is make yourself any more conspicuous than you already are," he had often said.

The building that hosted the Economic Forum for Small Business Opportunities was a nondescript three-story affair with reasonably fresh paint on its cindercrete-plastered walls. A small sidewalk sign announced the meeting taking place in Conference Room Five on the second floor.

She greeted the guard out front. He was busy fanning the coals underneath a small pot of tea.

"Good morning, miss," he said. "How are you this morning?"

"I'm fine. And you?"

"I'm also fine. I see by your nametag that you're here for the small business meeting. Second floor and to the right of the elevator. You might want to take the steps, though. The power comes and goes, as you probably know."

She did know. In her experience growing up in Bamako, it mostly went.

"Thank you," she said. "Have a good day."

"You too, miss."

Kyla knew that she was being addressed as miss out of respect, but she sometimes wished things weren't so formal.

She was early for the meeting but not the first to arrive. The short walk had her blood flowing and she gladly took a water bottle from the table. It had been sitting in a plastic tub of ice which was quickly turning into a swimming pool. She let the drops fall to the tile floor before twisting off the cap and letting the cool water soothe her parched throat. Even at nine in the morning, the heat could be significant in sub-Saharan Africa.

She heard a voice from behind her: "Good morning, Kyla."

Kyla turned and felt a flush of excitement at the sight of her friend. "Hey! Good morning, Maggie! I was wondering if I might see you here!"

The warmth of their shared hug energized Kyla more than the water. Maggie and Kyla had attended the same missionary school in Cote D'Ivoire and, thanks to social media, had been able to maintain contact over the years.

"So good to see you!" Maggie said. "I see you drew the short straw at your office too?"

"You got that right! I don't mind traveling… but I have to tell you, I can think of some other places I'd rather be. I better not say that too loud. Don't want to offend our hosts, you know."

"The heat can be a bit much, for sure."

"How was your trip?"

"Oh, you know, uneventful, I guess. Which is always good. All my luggage made it. That's always a bonus. How 'bout you?"

"Well, to be honest, I'm going to have a hard time focusing today. They somehow managed to misplace my pet dog, Scotty."

"Wait a minute. You brought along your pet dog?!"

"Well, that was the plan, yeah. But somehow the airline managed to lose him. My mind is going in a thousand different directions when I think about what could have happened to him. I *so* regret bringing him along, Maggs."

"Oh, man, I'm so sorry to hear that, Kyla. Have you been in touch with the airline?"

"Even better. I was so livid that the supervisor of the airport here in Ouaga has been in touch with his people in Bamako. He thinks Scotty may have been offloaded there. He promised to get back to me. If you see me getting up to go to the bathroom, it might just be to answer a phone call."

"Remember what your mom used to always say?"

"Yes, I do. 'God is not surprised by this.' Just once I wish God was surprised. Maybe then he'd get on top of fixing it."

"It'll work out, Kyla. You can't just lose a dog off the face of the planet. Scotty will show up."

"I hope you're right, Maggs. I do hope you're right."

Their conversation was interrupted by a smartly dressed young African man who suddenly walked up to them with his arm extended.

"Good morning," he said. "So glad you could join us. I'm Souleman Ahmad. I'll be leading the discussions this morning."

"Hello, Souleman. My name is Kyla Bouvier and this is my friend Maggie Langford."

"So pleased to meet you both. Tell me a little about yourselves."

"Well, Souleman, I work with Soin au Sahel in their regional office in Regina, Saskatchewan, Canada and Maggie here is from US International Help in Washington DC."

"Good. Well, welcome and I hope you enjoy your stay in Burkina Faso."

"Thank you. I'm sure we will," Kyla assured him.

Souleman slipped away to welcome some of the attendees who had just stepped through the meeting room doors.

"Why don't men in North America dress like that for meetings?" Maggie found herself saying aloud. "Would it kill them to put on some dress pants and shine their shoes once in a while?"

"It's true. Canada has become the true north, strong and casual."

The meeting was soon called to order.

After being introduced by Souleman, the keynote speaker, Tanner McFaden, spoke about how small-scale businesses could empower West African countries to take their place at the global economic table. He stood behind a ground-level dais at the front of the room while the attendees craned their necks to see.

Maggie and Kyla found themselves nodding and catching each other's eyes throughout the presentation. If only they could convince the big-time investors in Burkina Faso to take a chance on them! There was plenty of money in Burkina Faso, but those dollars were often linked to gold and other minerals. The focus was rarely on small business.

The real work began at the committee level in the afternoon. Maggie and Kyla were separated into different small groups. Their purpose was to brainstorm ways to encourage micro-enterprises in rural settings. Kyla heard a story about an NGO called This is Us (C'est Nous), a group of women who harvested mangos, cut and dried them, and packaged them for sale in bigger towns. After a modest initial investment in solar dryers and packing machines, the business had reached supersonic levels and their products had gotten wildly popular. They were poised to expand into cities like Bobo-Diallaso and Ouagadougou.

Kyla found herself drawn in to the discussions even though a part of her kept willing her phone to vibrate so she could find out the status of her pet Scotty.

It was not to be. The seminar ended for the day and Kyla caught up with Maggie at the coffee bar.

"Nothing says 'that's all, folks' like a piping hot coffee, n'est ce pas?" Maggie said cheerily.

"You got that right. Give me coffee or give me death!"

"Drama queen!" Maggie teased.

"Hey, I rocked at drama class. That has to be good for something."

"Yeah. Just look where it took your illustrious prime minister!"

"True, we may be the only country in the free world with a former drama teacher for a PM," Kyla said, keen to change the subject. "So what did you think of day one?"

"A good start. But you know what they say, right?"

"No, but I have a feeling I'm about to find out."

"You can lead a horse to water... but if you can make him dance, you've really got something."

Kyla laughed so hysterically that she immediately sought out the bathroom. Maggie had a way of making all the ugly parts of her day seem inconsequential.

They parted ways and promised to meet at 7:00 a.m. for an outdoor breakfast beneath the Touré Cafe sign near Kyla's hotel.

SCOTTY

I didn't sleep well. I kept wondering when my absence would be noted from the mud-walled storeroom.

In the muted light of predawn, I noticed a cooking pot sitting atop three well-placed rocks, the charred remains of some tree branches underneath. The sun was about to make her appearance beyond the mud walls of the yard.

I felt increasingly more nervous and whimpered to get Police's attention.

"Do you hear that?" I asked.

Police must have been emerging from a dream, because it took him a hot minute to respond.

"Hear what, little guy?"

"The commotion coming from the direction of that room where I dug myself out."

We both listened. Sure enough, there were raised human voices that sounded like alarm and consternation.

"You're right," he said. "They've probably noticed you aren't there."

"What should we do?"

"I like to do nothing until the situation unfolds. Then I do what comes naturally."

"Well, that might be how you roll, but I'm starting to feel mighty skittish."

"So what are you thinking?" Police asked.

"We both have four legs. I think it might be time to use them."

"Maybe you're right. Let's make ourselves scarce."

Word of my disappearance must have travelled fast. Before we could even run to the edge of the village, five big men in army fatigues and a collection of local boys were coming toward us. Police bounded off toward the town square and I tried my best to keep up. A stampede of barefoot boys in tattered T-shirts and shorts, each trying to shout louder than his mate, were determined to catch me. The entire village was on notice and I seemed to be the main event.

The boys were quicker than the men and they soon caught up. Suddenly, I heard a loud cracking noise, a sharp pain in my front leg, and I fell to the ground. One of the boys must have launched a big stick at me.

I couldn't move. Even as I lay on the ground, I tried to ward the boys off. My teeth must have made some of those boys think twice about grabbing me.

But eventually a grain sack tumbled over my head and it was all over. One minute I had been running and the next I was in a truck, wincing at every bump as my useless leg dangled awkwardly to one side.

Mercifully, the drive wasn't overly long. After throwing a device over my mouth that made it hard to breathe, a kind-looking lady attended to my wounded leg. She carefully ran her fingers down the leg and clicked the bone back into its original position. This was a new level of pain for me, but it somehow felt right to have the bone in place again. Then she placed two small sticks on each side of the leg and wrapped a kind of soft, stretchy material around it, making my leg feel secure. She poked me with something sharp that made me feel drowsy.

When I woke up, I was back in my kennel. I don't like to admit this, but I'd never felt happier to be in my own kennel than on that morning. It felt like I'd been sleeping for a week. I lapped up a lot of water from the dish in front of me. Where was I? What could be more bizarre than the last few days?

I just rested there, keeping an ear open to the sounds outside the big room where I was kept. I heard chickens and sheep coming and going. I didn't understand what any of this meant.

Before long, a leash was put around my neck and I was taken back outside. My leg already felt a bit better, and if I walked carefully I could put just the tiniest bit of weight on it.

The yard was surrounded by concrete walls. The only way to see out was through the small opening beneath a closed metal gate.

I rested under a stately mango tree and enjoyed the shade for a few minutes, recognizing the smell of burning charcoal and sweet tea. I had already associated that scent with visiting and laughter—and sure enough, a group of young men sat on stools around a small kettle. Kids occupied wooden benches with their parents. They pointed at me annoyingly and made noises that I could only presume were exclamations of surprise.

Frankly, I was getting tired of all the pointing, tongue-wagging, and laughter. To be fair, I probably did look unusual. I had way more hair than any native dog I had seen here. Smaller than any other dog too. So, all right, I guess I must have looked like a freak to these kids.

My thoughts were interrupted by a familiar bark. I also picked up the distinctive whiff of Police.

Nursing my leg, I hobbled over a little closer to the gate.

"Police, is that you?" I asked.

"Of course it's me," my friend's voice came back. "Who else would it be?"

"What are you doing here?"

"Never mind that. I have to bust you out of there. Is the torture bad in there? Are you bleeding?"

"They fixed my leg, Police. No torture. I'm not saying I'd want to spend my vacation here, but things could be worse."

"Forget that nonsense. I gotta bust you out before they do something really crazy!"

"Cool it, Police. Have you seen this place? The gate only opens for sick animals to come in and out. There's no way out."

"Says the beast who dug himself out of a locked room."

"Yeah, well, I'm not gonna be digging with only one front leg in working order."

"Listen, Nicky is here with me. We're gonna create a diversion. When the gate opens, run like your life depends on it—which it does, by the way."

"Hey, Nicky. Glad you guys could make it," I said. "What's the brilliant plan for a diversion?"

"We're working on that, little guy. Hang tight."

Before I could answer, I detected the smell of acrid smoke in the air. Flames leapt from a fifty-gallon barrel used for burning refuse. The wooden trusses beneath the tin roof of the building were already becoming scorched.

The gate swung open and several men ran outside. Moments later, they returned with a hose, frantically attempting to connect it to the spigot used for watering plants.

Without a second thought I burst through the gate and limped down the road after my new friends, red leash trailing behind me.

"Can you believe that?" Nicky exclaimed.

Police seemed astounded. "Our little buddy was busy creating the diversion without even letting us know. Brilliant!"

Diversion? Until a few minutes ago, I'd had no hope of ever making it out of that strange compound. Earlier I had seen a man sweeping up leaves and tossing them into the burning barrel. Something flammable must have ignited. I detected the strong odour of kerosene coming from the area around the rusty barrel.

But I didn't have time to explain all this to my friends.

"Shut up and run!" I shouted. "I'll follow!"

Sharp needles of pain shot up my leg every time it made contact with the reddish African dirt, but I did my best to keep my new comrades in sight.

I finally yelped for them to slow down. They stopped in the shade of a neem tree to wait.

"So what's the plan?" I ventured once I'd caught up and plopped myself down in the shade.

"Well, the first thing is to get your sorry butt off that donkey dung you're sitting in, unless you like rolling around in eau de crap," Nicky teased.

"Right now I could roll around in a fresh cow pie and think myself lucky," I said. "I'm alive. That's a bonus."

"Our little buddy's right," Police conceded. "Being a dog is no cakewalk. But right now we still have to come up with a plan."

Nicky had his head resting on his front paws, like he was ready to drift off to sleep. He raised his head. "I have an idea."

"This should be good," Police said sarcastically.

"Shut up and listen," Nicky countered. "What's the last place they would expect our little friend to run?"

Police was losing patience. "Nicky, I don't want to play 'chase the cat' here. We've got to get somewhere safe before the torture chamber people come to finish off our little furball."

"All right, don't get your whiskers in a dither. I think we should just head straight back to your place, Police. Let's be honest—your peeps feed you, give you water, and usually don't throw rocks and sticks your way. They might help, Scotty."

"I don't know. It's not my peeps I'm worried about," Police said. "It's the nutcase kids in the town. You saw what they did to Scotty here."

Scotty broke in. "Guys, if I might interject. There's no way I'm going back to the same place where they messed up my leg. No way. If that's the most brilliant plan you can think up, I'll just finish out my days here under this tree."

"Scotty, how far can you run on that gimpy leg?"

"I don't know. As long as I don't put much weight on it, I think I can run a fair piece."

"Look, here's the deal," Police said. "With so many of the female four-legs in heat now, my owners won't be surprised if I'm not around for one night. They'll just assume I'm busy making puppies. We could run to Sanankoroba."

"Sanankoroba! Sanankoroba? Are you nuts? Do you know how far that is?"

"It's not that far. Have you forgotten how to run, Nicky? I'm telling ya, it's not that far. If we do most of our travel tonight, we could be there by early morning."

"Police, I swear, sometimes I think you've swallowed one too many chicken bones." By now Nicky was sitting on his haunches. "We don't even know the lay of the land in Sanankoroba."

"Look, I don't know much about the town," Police said. "But I know there's a tubab lady there, and she just might have seen a little furball like Scotty in her day—"

"Are you guys forgetting that I'm right here?" I interrupted. "And what's a tubab lady?"

"A foreign woman… or man," Police explained. "They eat a lot of cheese and smell like milk. You're obviously not from around here and neither is she. Maybe she'll know what to do with you."

I felt a bit hurt. "You make it sound like I have a disease or something."

"Oh, don't get all soft on us, Scotty. You have to admit, you do stick out a bit. Listen, we're wasting time. I say we start making tracks to Sanankoroba right now."

"Police, chill your dog breath," Nicky countered. "How far ya think we're gonna get with our invalid friend here? Not to mention without food or water?"

"It rained the night before last, right?" Police asked.

"Yeah, so what?"

"So there's a nice little wadi around the halfway point. If we stick to the donkey cart path and stay off the main roads, we can have a nice drink there."

"Check out the sun, guys," I said. "We're lookin' at less than two hours before sunset. I'm with Police. I say we get moving. I just ate and drank water before you guys showed up. I'm good to go."

That was enough for Nicky and Police. After they got up and stretched, we all started on our journey.

We hadn't gone far when Police suddenly veered off the trail into some trees. Nicky and I followed him.

"Hang tight in here, guys," Police said. "I just smelled a donkey coming this way."

Sure enough, we soon saw a donkey pulling a cart with a dog running beside it.

"That's P.J.," Police whispered. "Coming back with firewood, by the looks of it."

"Won't he smell us?" I asked quietly.

"Of course he will. But if we stay in here and keep quiet, he'll ignore us."

Police was right. P.J. cast a glance in our direction but didn't bark. He was soon out of sight and we were able to get underway again.

"How did you know he wouldn't bark?" I asked.

"Simple. It's the West African code," Police stated, surprised that he would have to explain.

"West African code?"

"Yeah. Look, if I'm in the bush and I don't want attention, I exercise my right of first bark. If I don't bark, then neither does the approaching dog. It keeps us from a lot of undue attention from our two-legs."

"I like that system," I remarked. "Wish we had something like that where I'm from."

"Hey, how's the leg feelin'?" Police asked.

"It hurts like a bugger but I'll be okay."

"Good. We're not too far from the wadi. Hopefully P.J. hasn't muddied the water too much. He tends to wade right in to cool off. Can't seem to help himself."

True to Police's word, the wadi was a few minutes away, and I could smell the refreshment before I saw it. Surrounded by neem trees and a large mango tree, the wadi was full of freshwater. I knew better than to lap up too much water at once, but the effect of the water on my tongue was instantaneous. I hadn't realized how thirsty I was. Nicky and Police had their fill too.

As we journeyed on, my leg throbbed like a banshee, but I didn't complain. I just kept trotting along with my three good legs.

The smell of cooking fires, ochre, and boiled millet hung heavy in the air by the time we gained the outskirts of the village. I had smelled baking bread before, in Kyla's breadmaker, but the scent of a hundred cooking fires hammered my nostrils with an intensity I'd never experienced.

Sanankoroba. This was it. There was no turning back now.

"Okay, guys, so here's what we're gonna do," Police explained. "As appetizing as that food smells, we're gonna spend the night out here. No need to stir up a commotion. In the early morning light, we can make our way to the tubab's compound."

"Man, am I hungry," Nicky said.

Police growled. "Try to think of something other than your stomach, will ya? You're a one-dog eating machine."

"I do like me a good chicken bone now and again."

"That must be universal," I quipped. "It's hard to beat a good chicken bone."

But Police had put any thought of chicken bones to rest. Head lowered between forepaws, he was already snoozing, waiting for morning to come.

"Hey, Police?" I asked.

"Yeah."

"Sorry to wake you, but something's been bothering me and I just have to ask."

"Shoot."

"Why were those kids throwing sticks at me? I mean, that's never happened to me before."

"You must live in some kind of doggy paradise, my little friend. Did you notice that scar on Nicky's nose?"

"Hard not to."

"Right. Well, that trophy was from a stone pitched at him by his *master*. Not by some stranger who took exception to him, but by his bloody *owner*! So, yeah... stones, sticks, and just about every projectile you can imagine has been hurled our way at one time or another. It's just the way things are here. Fortunately, my two-legs is kind. I get fed half-decent food, and his kids let me rest. Speaking of which, maybe we should get some shuteye."

At that, I rested my head on my paws too.

It helped to understand that it wasn't just me, a stranger from the outside, who found himself on the end of occasional airborne objects.

My leg throbbed through the night, but I managed to rest a bit.

"Hey, sleepyheads, wake up!" It was Police, trying his best to growl quietly. "Follow me."

As I opened my eyes, he was already trotting toward the tubab's compound. No dog ever stirred just before daybreak, so our presence didn't alarm anydog.

"Now, Scotty, just so you know, Nicky and I aren't gonna' go into the compound," Police said. "You're gonna go in. I'm guessing that if our tubab friend is up, she'll take care of you. Me and Nick will make ourselves scarce. Got that? As soon as we see that she's noticed you—which she will, by the way—you won't see us again. It'll be easier, safer, and less complicated that way."

"What if she's not there?" I asked.

"Then you're in some serious kaka. But don't sweat it. She'll be there. Where else would she be?"

Police, who had already scoped the place out, nodded toward the open gate.

I hesitated.

"What are you waiting for?" Police asked. "Go, little guy. Trot right in there like you own the place."

A woman about Kyla's age emerged from the veranda carrying some water in a pail which she gently upended onto some plants in clay jars. That's when she spotted me.

When she called me over, I gingerly approached her, tail between my legs and looking as bedraggled as I could. Some gentle sounds came from her throat, the kind Kyla made after a bully dog had growled at me. The woman stroked my hair and fussed over my casted leg.

It sure did seem like I had fallen into the arms of a loving, caring person.

I glanced over to see if Police and Nick were anywhere outside, but of course they weren't. They were long gone, and it occurred to me that I hadn't even said thank you.

Kyla

"Wow," Maggie exclaimed after tasting her first sip of the coffee. "Not bad. Just like I remembered it. Ridiculously sweet with a large dose of caffeine. Some things never change."

"Right?" Kyla said. "I knew you'd like it here. And the ambience is unrivalled."

A honking van carrying passengers to another part of the city flew past, a young man hanging out of a doorless opening and waving his hands to urge pedestrians out of the van's path.

"Where else but in West Africa could you experience this?" Maggie asked rhetorically. "So you texted last night to say you had good news about Scotty. Sorry I didn't see it right away. I was already sleeping and my phone was off."

"The man from the airport phoned. I was just settling down to sleep when my phone rang. It was Mungolo Traoré from Bamako."

"What did he say?"

"Scotty is safe and sound and a kind family is taking care of him."

"Oh, Kyla, that's such good news! So he'll be on today's flight?"

"Well, that's apparently not going to happen."

"Why not?"

42

"Mr. Traoré said it had something to do with airline regulations about unaccompanied pets. He was running into all kinds of problems."

"So what does that mean for you?"

"It means they'll keep Scotty until I get to Bamako on Sunday. Then they'll put him in the cabin with me back to Paris."

"Well, good for you! You must be relieved," Maggie said.

"Yes and no. When I asked a few more questions about the family that was looking after Scotty, Mr. Traoré seemed to grow evasive. But you have to trust people, right?"

"Of course you do."

"It's funny, because minutes before Traoré's call I sent out a 'lost dog' notice on a Facebook page. I know Scotty isn't technically *lost*, but I just felt like I had to do something. I even posted a picture of my little guy, along with the whole crazy story of how he came to be misplaced."

"Nothin' wrong with that. I know how it is. You feel like you have to do something, right?"

"Exactly. Fourteen people already liked my post."

"You'd be surprised how many people are scrolling through their social media feeds at work."

"Guilty as charged. Who hasn't done that?"

"Hey, what time does our session start today?" Maggie asked, suddenly changing the subject. "I feel like it's a later start for some reason."

"Yes, It's 10:30. I think it had something to do with the facilitator having another appointment."

"Want to come back to my place? We can grab a decent breakfast."

"What, and miss out on this place with the flies buzzing around the jam jar?"

"Shhh! Do you want to offend Touré?"

"I don't think he would be the least bit offended," Kyla assured her. "My dad has a great story. He was riding along with some pastors to a meeting when they stopped for lunch at one of those outdoor straw hangar places beside the buses. They walked into one, saw the lack of hygiene, and almost walked right back out again. The proprietor asked, 'You're not staying?' One of the pastors replied, 'I can afford your food. I just can't afford the medicine I would need to recover from eating it.'"

"No way! A pastor said that!?"

"They can be incredibly tactful and diplomatic. But they can be brutally honest too."

On the walk to Maggie's hotel, a young boy offered to carry their bags, fetch things from the market, and help them find their way to wherever they were going. He followed them for several blocks and then decided they weren't worth his time.

As they walked along, Maggie marvelled at the bolts of colourful cloth atop one man's head.

"Some of that stuff looks pretty decent," she remarked. "Do you remember the market in Bouake? I loved seeing all that mud cloth and tie-dye stuff."

"I know. If I had more of an allowance, I would have bought so much of that stuff. But by the time I bought all the soda and candy, there wasn't much left for clothes."

44

"Do you remember what Aunt Michelle always said to us?"

"How could I forget?" Kyla scrunched up her face to look older and serious. "Man looks at the outward appearance, but the Lord looks at the heart."

They both laughed.

"Honestly, Kyla, our time at ICA sometimes felt like an ongoing Sunday school class."

ICA was short for the Ivory Coast Academy, an on-campus school where she and Maggie had spent three years together.

"You were a bit of a rebel, as I recall," Kyla observed.

"Me? Boy crazy, maybe, but I mostly followed the rules."

"Of which there were plenty."

"Every rule is there for a reason. The rules are your friends. Remember how often Aunt Beth would say that?"

"One too many times for my taste," Maggie agreed. "But I get it. Now that I'm older, I put myself in our dorm parents' shoes and wonder how they didn't lose their minds with all those hormones piled up in one place."

"Right? I mean, talk about frustration. Your heart is head-over-heels in love, you can't think of anything else all day long, but you're not allowed to be together, let alone kiss your true love."

"Ah, young love." Maggie sighed wistfully. "The way of love never did run smooth."

"Don't you mean, the *river* of love never did run smooth?" chided Kyla.

"Hey, don't get all 'Professor Kyla' on me. At least I know it's a quote from one of Willy's plays."

"*A Midsummer Night's Dream*, to be precise."

"Look who knows so much! I never liked Shakespeare. *The Old Man and the Sea* was more my style. And speaking of style, here we are!"

They had arrived at Maggie's hotel. Apparently US International Help was a bit more flush with money than Soin au Sahel. Kyla snuck a glance at the pool, tastefully shaded with palm trees next to the seven-foot stone fence enclosure. Several chaise lounges were lined up invitingly on either side of the pearl-shaped, sky-blue pool. At this time of the morning it looked stunningly tranquil.

Kyla had just been happy that Soin au Sahel had booked her into a hotel with hot and cold running water.

"Wow, this place is amazing!" Kyla gushed.

"Wait till you see my room."

The room was indeed beautiful. The curtains were drawn and the indirect sunshine cast shadows across a perfectly made king-sized bed. A spiral notebook and laptop lay on top of a long waist-high shelf with a padded chair pushed to the side.

"Mind if I use your bathroom?" Kyla asked.

"Of course not. Go crazy."

The bathroom too was a marvel of West Africa. The shower looked like it had been tiled yesterday. Apart from the towel Maggie had flung over the countertop, all the other towels were hung in perfect order.

Kyla emerged from the bathroom. "Okay. You've officially arrived, girl. How can US International Help afford to put you up here?"

"I'm guessing because they're the largest aid organization on the planet. I don't think three nights in this place is going to even make a dent in their bottom line." Maggie was browsing through the brochures for the upcoming session. "Hey, I just had an idea."

"Uh-oh! Maggs has had an idea. This could be dangerous."

"Why don't you just move in here with me for the duration of the conference?" Maggie suggested.

"I can think of a lot of reasons, not the least of which is how I would explain the additional bill to my boss when I got home."

"What bill? As far as they're concerned, you're still in the other place."

"True, but there's only one bed," Kyla pointed out.

"King Tut's bed, yeah. Honestly, I don't think we would find each other in this bed… even if we wanted to."

"It would make things a lot simpler, given that the conference is right here and all," Kyla admitted. "Are you sure I wouldn't be putting you out?"

"Please, Kyla. I could use the company." After hearing no further objections, Maggie blurted out, "It's decided then! After the meeting today, go get your stuff and we'll be roomies. End of story."

Kyla heard her phone ping with that familiar sound she associated with Facebook notifications.

"Hey, what's the wifi password here?" Kyla asked.

Maggie handed her the folded card from the end table.

"No way!" Kyla exclaimed when she'd opened the app to a picture of Scotty. "Maggie, take a look at this."

"Is that your dog? He's so cute!"

"Yeah, but that's not what's interesting. Look at this comment…"

Maggie took the phone and read aloud. "'Hey, I think I know something about your dog. Please message me back.'" Maggie handed the phone back to Kyla. "What's up with that?"

"I don't know, but I intend to find out."

"Careful, Kyla," Maggie warned. "It could be a scam."

"Let me look at this girl's profile. It says here that she works for the Feet of Peace in Sanankoroba, Mali. That's really close to Bamako. I'm gonna message her back."

"Does her profile look legit?

"Nothing out of the ordinary."

Kyla typed out a quick reply to the woman and sent it off. Almost immediately her phone dinged with a response.

"Well?" Maggie was almost as excited as Kyla, but Kyla was too busy tapping away with her two thumbs to answer.

Kyla pursed her lips in concentration. "Well, surprises never cease!"

"What?"

"She asks how unreliable my internet is here. She's gonna phone me in a few minutes. Says she's pretty sure she has my dog."

"What! Could it be true?"

"I sure hope so."

And with that, she heard the ringtone of a phone call. Voice only, no video. She doubted that the woman on the other end would have the bandwidth to do a video conference.

"Hello," the woman began. "Is this Kyla?"

"It sure is. Talk to me, Sandra. You think you have my dog?"

"This morning, just as I was watering my plants on the veranda, I saw a little dog, a Scottish terrier like the one on your Facebook

48

post, coming through my gate. He was really shy at first, but he soon warmed up to me. Does your dog have a bandaged right front leg?"

"No, he doesn't. Or at least he didn't when we boarded our flight in Paris."

"He's got a collar with a tag on it that says 'Scotty 91765.'"

Kyla nearly dropped the phone.

"Kyla? Are you still there?"

Kyla was a sobbing, slobbering mess, but she managed to pull herself together. "Yes, Sandra, I'm here. You have Scotty all right. That's his tag. He's registered with that number. Did you say he had a sore leg?"

"Yes. It looks like someone has taken care of it for him. He might have tried to chew off some of the gauze, but it looks like he's pretty much left it alone. I can change out the dressing if you want me to."

"Could you, Sandra? That would be so kind. It's so weird because they told me at the airport that he was with a family and they would take care of him until I got there."

"Who told you this?" Sandra asked.

Maggie suddenly shoved a handwritten message in front of Kyla: *Off to the meeting. I'll tell them you were unexpectedly delayed.*

Kyla managed to nod to her friend as she answered Sandra's question. "Mr. Traoré from the Airport Authority in Bamako. He said he couldn't work things out with the airline for Scotty to be shipped to Ouaga, but they would keep Scotty safe…"

"All right, Kyla, listen to me. If they ever had Scotty in their pos-session, he's obviously not there now because he's with me. If they

49

did manage to lose your little guy, which seems likely, Mr. Traoré probably didn't want to be the bearer of bad news. So instead he bought time by hiding the truth. In any case, I don't think we can trust these people, do you?"

Kyla appreciated the calm assurance she heard in Sandra's voice; it was such a contrast to the freaked-out nature of her own heart. "Maybe not."

"Listen, how long are you in Ouaga?"

"I was supposed to fly out on Sunday."

"Can you change your ticket?"

"I think so."

"Did you buy insurance with your ticket?"

"Yes. What are you thinking?"

"Change your ticket to fly home by way of Abidjan. There are flights out of Ouaga every day to Abidjan. I'm gonna bring Scotty to you."

"What? Sandra, you're not making any sense. Why would we do all this? Why can't you just keep him there and take him to the Bamako Senou airport on Sunday when my flight comes in?"

"Right into the lap of our friend, Mr. Traoré? Kyla, if Traoré screwed up this badly, he's going to pull out all the stops to find Scotty. It's only a matter of time before the trail leads to me. Based on how well they took care of Scotty the first time, I think he'll be safer with me."

"You have a point there."

"I have a multiple entry visa to Burkina Faso and could easily jump on a bus and meet you at the bus depot in Ouaga. I promise I'll bring Scotty to you safe and sound."

"I think I like you, Sandra. You seem like a kind person. Where are you from in the States?"

"I didn't say I *was* from the States. Why would you think I'm American?"

"Two things. One, I was creeping your Facebook page. And two, I hear a Midwest accent."

"That obvious, huh?"

"Yup."

"I'm from Kansas City, Missouri. Go Chiefs!"

Kyla laughed at that. "Mahomes is pretty cute, I'll grant you that."

"You got that right! I'm surprised you would know about it, being from the Great White North and all."

"So you were creeping me too?" Kyla asked with a chuckle.

"Absolutely. Can't be too careful, you know."

"This whole thing seems too bizarre to be true."

"I know. Listen, you probably have things to do… and so do I. If you really are okay with the plan, I'm gonna buy my ticket ASAP. If all goes well, I should arrive later tonight. Are you okay with meeting me at the bus depot?"

"Of course! I'd walk across the Sahara to see Scotty again. I'll have my phone charged and with me at all times. Just keep me posted."

"Gotta love West Africa, huh?" Sandra noted.

"And Facebook. Don't forget Facebook." Kyla hesitated for a moment. "Hey, Sandra?"

"Yeah?"

"Thank you. I don't know how I can ever repay you."

"Repay me? Nothin's happened yet. A lot of things need to line up for us to pull off this plan. Do you pray, Kyla?"

"Wow! That question kind of came out of nowhere."

"In North America, the question would be unusual… but here in West Africa, it's pretty normal. So do you?"

"To be honest, Sandra, I haven't prayed for a long time."

"Well, now might be a good time to start. Like I said before, a lot of pieces have to fall together to pull this off. Prayer sure wouldn't hurt." A moment passed. "I don't have a kennel, Kyla. Do you think Scotty would bolt on me if he got scared?"

"I don't think so. But if you could fashion a leash for him and attach it to his collar, that would help. It'll make it easier if he does try to run. How does he seem?"

"Oh, he's comfortable, apart from that sore leg. In fact, he's sitting on my lap right now."

"That's so good to hear! I can't tell you how much it means to me that he's not stressed out."

"You're probably more stressed out than he is right now," Sandra said. "When I get closer to Ouaga, I'll text you and you can meet me at the bus depot."

"Sounds good, Sandra. I should probably get to my meeting and try to sound coherent. See you later. Safe travels."

"Okay. Bye."

SCOTTY

Trust is a hard thing to explain. For reasons unknown even to me, I implicitly knew this lady would be kind and caring. Maybe it was a familiar smell. Police told me I smelled like cheese and crackers… I had no idea what he meant by that, but this lady had a familiar smell to her that put me in mind of Kyla. She stroked my fur and spoke to me soothingly, just like Kyla did. I felt at home, if that's possible in a place where the sun's as hot as a furnace and dust from passing donkey carts and cars fills your nostrils.

The kind lady carried me into a small mud room off her veranda, flicked on a dim light, and set me down gently on a table. I had no thoughts of running. I felt safe.

She peeled off the bandage on my leg and it hurt a bit, especially when some of the fur came off with the encrusted blood. She put something warm and wet on my leg, then dried it off and rewrapped it with that same stretchy material as before.

Next, she gave me some water and rice. It felt so good to be able to eat something and I felt my strength return.

As I ate, I heard some tapping from a table. The lady seemed to be hitting something with her fingers just like I'd seen Kyla do back in Regina. She lowered a short rope around my neck, which worried me a bit, but continued to talk to me soothingly. She tied the other end of the rope to the leg of a wooden table and went into another room. I heard the rustling sound of clothing being thrown into a bag. Again, it reminded me of what Kyla did whenever she and I were going on a trip for a few days.

The lady soon came back into the room and loosened my rope. She gathered me up and held me in the crook of one arm, slinging the bag over her other shoulder.

The two of us climbed into the back seat of a noisy car.

As the day passed, it was just her, me, and the driver traveling along a road. I would have stuck my head out the window to gulp down some air, but after watching the lady try unsuccessfully to move a handle on the door, I assumed the window of this particular car didn't work.

We came to a busy, chaotic place with people everywhere. The lady deftly picked me up with one hand and pulled some paper out of her pocket with the other. She gave the paper to the man who had been behind the wheel of the car and then we approached a large line of huge machines, some of them spewing smoke.

The lady approached a man standing behind a wooden counter. They exchanged some papers, and all the while I just tried to keep quiet, even though I saw a dog trot by who bore an insane resemblance to Police.

After receiving her papers, my caretaker sat down on a metal chair. I grew sleepy watching all the other people exchange papers with the man behind the counter…

I'd barely closed my eyes when she gathered me up in her arms to board the bus. We were ready to go! The lady and the man at the door of the bus were having a loud discussion. He kept pointing at me and then to a big door on the bus's side. The lady was shaking her head.

Finally, the lady pulled some more paper from her pocket and gave it to the man, who motioned with his hand that we should get in.

The lady walked down a long aisle and sat in a chair, placing me on her lap. We both tried to avoid getting squished by the large man sitting next to us. He wore a large coat which he kept adjusting. No doubt he was trying to get comfortable. Why anyone would be wearing a coat in a roaster like we had just climbed into was beyond me.

I eventually succumbed to sleep.

At one point, I thought the trip was over. Everyone got off the bus, including us. She put me on the ground next to some bushes and I emptied my bladder. Then she lowered herself beside me and I heard some tinkling sounds. I guess we had some things in common. Kyla had done that once when we were beside a lake, far away from people.

We got back on the bus and I soon fell asleep in the lady's lap again. I had no idea where we were going, but it seemed like a good idea to bank a few hours of sleep before we got there.

In that space between wakefulness and deep sleep, I heard a thumping sound from underneath us. The bus began to slow, and eventually it stopped altogether. Everyone went outside, squatting beside the road and looking for shade. No one seemed to be in the least bit uptight.

The lady put me down on the ground and I gingerly took a few steps to keep limber. We sheltered beneath a delightfully shady tamarisk tree in the lengthening shadows of the late afternoon.

I watched some men with big metal tools remove a round object from beneath the bus. After an hour or so, and many grunts and raised voices, the men shouted something and soon we were all finding our seats again. The lady picked me up and carried me to where we had been sitting.

We were soon moving, with the big man next to us pinning the lady's shoulder to the window. I truly felt sorry for her because she seemed to be in considerable discomfort. I was just glad to sit safely on her lap. Whatever was going to happen, I felt sure I would be okay with her.

Kyla

When Kyla finished her call with Sandra, she returned to the conference and joined Maggie in the seat her friend had saved for her. Kyla tried gamely to sit down unnoticed, and luckily the speaker was just drawing on his flipchart at the far end of the table and didn't see her slip in.

"You look like the cat who ate a mouse," Maggie whispered.

"Isn't that 'the cat who swallowed a canary'?"

"Whatever! You look very happy. What did you find out?"

"I'll tell you later. I think we better pay attention to the meeting right now," Kyla said quietly as the speaker turned to face the conference attendees.

The presenter was dressed smartly in navy blue pants, a white long-sleeved shirt, and a muted red tie. His hair had been cropped short and his eyeglasses gave him a distinctly Malcolm X look. His smooth voice added to his allure and Kyla found herself drawn inexorably to the information he delivered.

Beside him was a chart demonstrating the profits of a particular micro-enterprise focused on cultivating and selling tomatoes in local markets in Bobo-Diallasso. The chart showed two years of modest growth followed by a spike in profits that only plateaued after an astonishing 180 percent growth rate.

"This is possible," he was explaining, "because these women do not have to use any of their money to bribe officials, or to pay husbands or relatives, which would most certainly be the case if men were running this enterprise. The money is put into the cooperative and bills are paid, with substantial profits shared equally among the women involved. And trust me, no husband in his right mind has any objections to what they're doing—because as leaders in their own households, they've seen nothing but a positive economic impact financially. Where they struggled to pay for books and supplies for their school-aged children, they now find that they can purchase all these items and still have money left over at the end of each month. But I'm starting to see that glazed-over look in your eyes. Let's take a ten-minute break. Then we'll talk about how something like this might look for the organizations you represent."

Kyla went straight to the orange juice laid out in little plastic cups on a table close to the door. Maggie was soon at her elbow.

"Well?"

"Well what?" Kyla teased, knowing that Maggie must be bursting with curiosity.

"Don't do this, Kyla. Out with it already!"

"Well, she's on her way to Ouaga as we speak. And she has Scotty!"

"What? Are you serious?"

"Yup. She convinced me to let her do this. Trust me, I didn't ask her. She said that it would be foolish to trust Mr. Traoré after he lied to me."

"How do you feel about that?" Maggie asked.

"At first, I wasn't sure. But West African culture being what it is, Traoré wouldn't want to admit that his people lost Scotty. He would double down his resources, move heaven and earth to find him, and find any way he could to stall. I mean, does it surprise me that this happened? Not a bit. But after I thought about it, I couldn't shake the feeling that this wasn't simply a case of messing up. Scotty was injured because of their neglect. He could die in their care. So, yes, I trust a dog-lover more than the authorities at this point."

"So Sandra's on her way here. How? Surely not on the plane."

"No. Sounds like she knows her way around public transit. She'll be on a bus. She'll text me when the bus gets a bit closer. I'm supposed to meet her at the station. It won't be until evening at the earliest."

Maggie put her hand on Kyla's shoulder. "This is great news, huh?"

"Absolutely it is. The only downside is that I have to change my flight. I'll fly to Abidjan instead of going through Bamako."

"You can't just stick to the flight you've already booked?"

"And risk more problems in Bamako? Think about it. Traoré will want to put this to rest. The last thing he wants is a disgruntled passenger fanning the flames of social media with a story about how the Bamako Airport Authority lost a dog. And local media outlets are relentless in finding stories just like this to shame the authorities. I mean, he might not care. Maybe he'll just hope he never sees me again. But that's not a chance I'm prepared to take."

"Well, changing your ticket shouldn't be too hard, right? Did you buy insurance?"

"I did," said Kyla.

"So apart from the hundred bucks they'll charge you for changing your ticket, it should work."

"We can take care of it back in your room when the meeting is done."

The meeting was in fact ready to reconvene and the participants were taking their seats. The next speaker, Drissa Kabore—Kyla had surreptitiously scrolled through the notes on her phone to find the presenter's name—divided the participants into three tables of three people each. Each was to appoint a leader, take notes, and be prepared to share ideas on their organizations' goals and challenges.

"Don't be afraid to go wild here," Kabore said. "And don't make any judgments. Just put your ideas out there. Sometimes the ideas that seem craziest end up working out."

For the next hour, Kyla scrambled to record all her group's thoughts. Although they talked about many challenges, she was heartened to hear about all the small-scale ventures that worked. New ideas flew in like locusts: fishing tourism, cycling tours, mobile health clinics, movie-making… the list got long.

Throughout the session, she made a Herculean effort to push away thoughts of Scotty. Where was he now? Was he all right? Would his leg withstand a long trip? Would she be able to find the train station at night?

It was coming up on five o' clock when Kyla and Maggie got back to the hotel room, flung down their bags, and kicked off their shoes.

A flurry of texts awaited Kyle when she checked her phone.

"On our way! Everything good." Then, three hours later: "Crap. Flat tire. No spare, of course. This could be a while." And the most recent one: "On our way again. One of the men caught a ride back to the last town we passed through and came back with a different tire. Gotta love W.A."

She had been in enough situations to remember that West Africans always seemed to find a way.

"Well, what's the news?" Maggie asked.

"A few hiccoughs, but they're on their way."

"Any idea when they might arrive?"

"Not really. The bus usually takes between twelve and thirteen hours, but that's if everything goes smoothly."

"Which it rarely does in West Africa."

"Tell me about it! Apparently they had a flat tire and the bus company didn't have the foresight to have a spare on hand."

Maggie shrugged. "Who needs a spare tire? The signs on these buses usually say something like 'L'homme propose, Dieu Dispose.'"

"Exactly. And if God is controlling the fate of the trip, why interfere? Anyway, they should be here by eleven o'clock tonight. I can't wait to see my little guy."

"In the meantime, don't you think you should change your ticket?" Maggie asked.

"Yes. Thanks for reminding me. It'll keep me from going crazy."

"And while you're working on that, I'll go downstairs and see what the buffet looks like. We might want to go out for supper if they're serving fish again."

"You don't like fish, Maggs?"

"Not my personal favourite, no."

Kyle closed her eyes for a moment, calling back a childhood memory. "We had this fish growing up in Mali called *capitaine*. As fish go, it was the closest thing to a juicy steak you'll ever eat. Tender, white, fleshy meat with almost no bones. I'm getting hungry just describing it."

"You're not tempting me, Kyla. Now get busy with those tickets."

"Do you think I should wait until Scotty's back?"

"Why? You don't think this lady from Sanankoroba is on the level?" Maggie asked.

"Oh, I trust her. I just know that things can go sideways in a hurry on public transport. They've already had one flat tire. What if the engine on this mechanical marvel stops altogether?"

"You're overthinking things. Why don't you fire off a text and see if she responds?"

"Good idea. Now go check out the buffet."

Maggie left the room and Kyla started typing out a text.

Sandra's response was almost immediate. They had already crossed the Mali-Burkina border. Scotty was fine, sleeping contentedly on Sandra's lap. Eleven o'clock still seemed like a reasonable arrival ETA.

Maggie returned from her mission to find Kyle sitting on the bed with her laptop out. "Fish and more fish. Not much else out there, Kyla. How're you doing with those airline tickets?"

"Not bad. I found the credit card in your purse and used that. Hope you don't mind."

"Ha! Very funny. A regular Nate Bargatze, you are."

"Boom! Done!" Kyla exclaimed as she hit some keys on the laptop. "I'm on my way to Abidjan."

"What about Scotty? Can you take him in the cabin this time?"

"Apparently yes, but he has to have a special little kennel that sits at my feet. I guess I'll have to cruise the markets for a suitable carry-on."

Maggie sighed. "It's always something."

"Hey, I don't mind. If I have to scour through every market in Ouagadougou, I'll do it. Anything to avoid what happened last time."

"So when do you fly out?" Maggie asked.

"Saturday afternoon. Once I'm in Abidjan, I have three hours before the flight to Paris. Another two and half hours in Paris and then I'm on to Pearson in Toronto. Should be enough time between flights, eh?"

"Lots of time. No customs in Paris. Just hanging out in the passenger lounge. I like to leave a few hours between flights just in case the planes out of Africa are late taking off."

Kyla put the laptop away. "Which they sometimes are. One time my family and I were seated in the plane at Bamako, ready to go back to Regina. I was so excited to see my grandma and grandpa and all my cousins. But we just sat on the tarmac. All of a sudden, we see a fancy white Mercedes-Benz pull up right beside the plane. Three men jump out, climb the staircase, and get on the plane, each wearing a fancy white jemeez. Must have had some connections with the government. Still, I was fuming. Like, you dudes couldn't have arrived on time and gone through the airport customs like everyone else? And If you're gonna get special treatment, at least have your chauffeur arrive on time!"

"Crazy. So how much of a delay are we talking about?"

"Oh, probably only ten minutes, but I was not a happy camper. I had cousins to see!"

"Absolutely! I know exactly what you mean." Maggie chuckled to herself. "Hey, if you're all done we should go find some food. There's a nice restaurant down the block."

"I'm famished."

Kyla was glad to have her friend by her side. Maybe everything would work out.

The restaurant they ended up at, La Riviere Bleue, was nearly empty when they arrived—and they were serving Thai food. In West Africa, it was rare to eat supper before seven o'clock. Their table was in the corner, a slender branch of a fig tree spilling out near them from a massive flower pot beside their booth.

"So let me ask you a question," Maggie began. "If you had known Scotty would get lost, that all this craziness would happen, would you have brought him?"

"Way to pour lemon juice in the wound, Maggs. Of course I wouldn't have. I would've dropped him off at his favourite kennel—a kennel, by the way, that he treats like his own personal spa. Don't think I haven't thought about this every minute of the last few days. You always ask such tough questions! You should have gone into counselling or something."

"I might just do that yet. But think about it. As much as we like to think we're in control of our lives, things can be so dang random. It's like we have almost zero say in what happens to us sometimes, ya know?"

Kyla nodded vigorously. "Oh, I know. I never could have predicted that I'd be sitting at a Thai restaurant in Ouagadougou, talking to a girlfriend I haven't seen in years, waiting for my dog to travel on a bus with a lady I've never met. Yup. Life can be random sometimes."

"This is changing the subject, but do you see yourself working for Soin au Sahel a long time? Like, is this your career now?"

"Honestly, Maggie, I couldn't tell you. I mean, I like my job. My supervisor is great. I'm appreciated and I get encouragement, but I don't see myself doing this long-term."

"I'm glad they're treating you well. The minute that changes, you gotta move on."

"Sounds like that's coming from the voice of experience," Kyla commented.

"Yeah. I wish I was appreciated at work. I mean, I guess no one is breathing down my neck to get things done, but I feel like a small cog in a giant wheel, ya know? Like I could disappear and it would be a while before anyone even noticed."

"Ants Marching, right?"

"I didn't know you were a Dave Matthews fan. I love that song."

"Yeah. Sometimes it does seem like we're all pawns in a giant chess game."

"Well, I hate chess, but life can feel pointless at times. There has to be an organizing structure of some kind, doesn't there? Lately, I've been wondering if God is out there after all."

"So... is he?" Kyla asked.

"I haven't been to church since my girlfriend got married last summer. I feel like I've been drifting away from whatever faith I had."

"So, for you, God is out there… but he's not personal?"

"He might be. I'm not sure what I think about a personal relationship with God, and why oh why does it seem so much easier to talk about God in Africa than back home? Can you tell me that?"

"It's because the spiritual is real here, Maggie. It's not some philosophical construct, a topic to avoid at office parties. Everyone in this part of the world knows God is real. It's a truth with virtually universal acceptance. Did I tell you what Sandra said?"

"What did she say?"

"She asked me if I prayed. Said now might be a good time to start."

"Well, she's not wrong, Kyla. So what did you tell her?"

"Nothing really. The conversation moved on to buses and whatnot."

"So do you?"

"Do I what?"

"Come on, Kyla. Track with me here. Do you pray?"

"Last month, my parents had me over for supper. Dad asked me to say grace. I did. I know the right words to say. It's like muscle memory. But I'm not sure it means anything. Let's face it, Maggs, I've drifted—or, in the words of my mom, I've backslid."

Maggie nodded, able to relate. "Walked away from the Lord."

"Turned my back on faith."

"At least you're not living in sin."

By now, the two women were laughing at all the Christian clichés.

"You know what's funny, Maggs?" Kyla said. "It seems like there are more clichés about people who aren't walking the straight and narrow than people who are."

"On fire for the Lord, in close fellowship with Jesus, sold out for their faith, all in…?" Maggie ventured.

"Okay. Point taken. Maggie, do you remember those trips we would take in the van on Friday nights to villages around Bouake?"

"How could I forget? It was our one chance to get off-campus to see some authentic village life."

"Well, one time our group went to Bouafle. I was so pumped because I got to sit beside Terry, and I'm pretty sure he liked me… but I digress. Anyway, we got to the village, started setting up — you know, the big portable screen, the film projector, all that stuff. We had just gathered in front of this large rectangular mud house and a pretty good crowd had gathered. The boys were finished setting up the equipment and had done some sound tests."

"Allo, allo, test, test, test," Maggie cut in.

"Couldn't resist, could you?" Kyla smiled at the memory. "Anyway, if I may return to my story? Out of the corner of my eye, I saw what I can only describe as a witch."

"A witch? Seriously?"

"I'm dead serious. She had tangled hair, her boobs were showing through a ragged shirt, her skirt was barely hanging around her waist, and she was screaming!"

"Screaming?"

"Screaming, yes. Like no language I had ever heard before. A high-pitched wailing, and then a man's voice came out of her mouth. I tell you, Maggs, sometimes I still see her in my nightmares. We started singing 'Nothing But the Blood of Jesus,' I believe."

"*Fen si te fo Yesu Joli,*" Maggie said.

"Wow. Where did you pull that out of?"

"Give me some credit, Kyla. My memory is decent."

"So we started singing, and that lady settled right down," Kyla continued. "She sat where she was and soon the pastors were talking to her. This was happening at the back of the crowd, but I saw them praying for her. I'll never forget that. Some kind of power was flowing out of our words, Maggie."

"That is so cool. So what do you make of all that?"

"I guess I'm just sayin' there has to be power in praising God, because that's what we were doing. We were raising our voices in praise about the power of Jesus's blood. Was it a coincidence that the lady settled down just then? I doubt it. There must be things happening in the spiritual realm that we have no idea about."

"So where does all that leave you?"

"I guess I'm open and curious, Maggie. You?"

"Oh, this isn't about me."

"Of course it is. I just shared things I haven't spoken about for twenty years," Kyla said. "I want to hear where you're at."

"I'm kind of like you in some ways."

"Don't tell me—another backslider in our midst?"

"If going to church is what it's all about, I'm in serious trouble," Maggie said. "My parents don't talk to me about it much, but I can tell they're worried about my 'spiritual condition.'"

"I hear you, sister."

"A few years ago, I moved in with a guy. They were none too happy, let me tell you. My mom was disappointed and told me so. My dad? Well now, that was a different matter."

"What did he say?"

"*Maggie…*" She affected a deep voice and serious manner. "*…you are making a serious mistake. I thought you had better judgment than that. The Lord is not mocked, Maggie. You can't live in sin and expect to go unpunished.*"

Kyla nodded along. "But that was a few years ago. Where do things stand now?"

"Well, Damion and I split up. He wasn't good for me, Kyla. He was suffocating me, expecting so much and not contributing anything. I caught him making out with a lady friend on a park bench, and that evening I tossed his things onto the lawn and told him to never come back, at least not if he knew what was good for him. So in a way, I guess my dad was right. I had poor judgment…" She trailed off, switching to a different memory. "Anyway, there was this girl from my office who was so kind. You know those people who are super good listeners but don't hammer you with advice?"

"Yeah, I wish I knew more of them," said Kyla. "Most people listen with a mind to throw in their two cents as soon as you've finished a sentence."

"Exactly! Well, Mel was her name—technically Melanie, but she wanted us to call her Mel. Anyway, she came to the bar with us after work one Friday. Most everyone left around 6:30, leaving just me and Mel. She listened to my sob story about Damion and from the way she was listening I just knew she could feel my pain. Long story short, she invited me to a church group she met with on Tuesday nights. I figured, why not? Mel had been there for me when others weren't. I know this sounds mercenary, but I figured I owed it to her, ya know?"

"What was this group like?"

"I mean, they talk about God, about how he's helping them in their daily lives. They usually read some verses from the Bible and pray… but hey, I'm used to that from school, right?"

"Every night, if your dorm was the same as ours."

"Every night is right," said Maggie. "Followed by night lunch. It was usually worth the investment."

"Good investment, indeed. It was also a time to use words for personal agendas."

"Meaning?"

"Well, I remember one time Uncle Dave asked me to pray. I thought to myself, 'Wow, Kyla, a few minutes ago you were swearing at your roommate for rifling through your stuff, and now you're supposed to be all Mother Teresa-like?' So I prayed that we would all respect each other and give one another space. Needless to say, Aunt Brenda figured something was up with that prayer and came to talk to me alone later. I really loved Aunt Brenda. She had a sense about that kind of thing. Anyway, back to your weird church group."

"They're some of the most loving, caring people I know."

Kyla felt herself growing sceptical. "Sure, until you mess up. Then get ready for the tanks to come out."

"I get why you might say that, but I don't think these friends would act that way. I mean, they all know I was living with Damion without being married to him."

"Yes, living in sin."

"You got that right," Maggie said with a humorless laugh. "If he hadn't moved out, it would have been first-degree murder and I'd be in jail right now. I was so mad. But I came to see that I was building my value around his approval. I wanted someone to fall head over heels in love with me, to feel valued."

"Valued, eh? Trust me, I've been there."

"You'll probably mock me, but…"

"No mocking, I promise."

"One night, we were talking about what God is like. They were kind of going around the circle, each one talking about what God meant to them, and I realized it was gonna be super awkward when I had nothing to offer. Because really, Kyla, at that moment in my life I was as dry as a twig in the desert. So I just said, 'I'll pass.'"

Kyla sighed. "Exactly what I would have done."

"At work the next day, Mel pulled me aside and said, 'I hope that wasn't too awkward for you last night.' So I lied: 'Not at all.' Then she proceeded to tell me that she talked to the leader after the meeting to tell him that going around the circle like that may not have been the best idea."

"Sounds like this lady has some horse sense."

"Lots of it. Anyway, we went out for coffee after work and I told her everything: my fears, my frustrations, my disappointment with God… I didn't hold anything back. And right there in that coffee shop, Mel prayed for me. It was the most beautiful prayer I'd ever heard. I felt God smiling on me that day. I didn't feel like a big old policeman was just waiting for me to mess up. I just felt His love."

Maggie paused to let her friend respond.

"So you rededicated your life to the Lord?" Kyla ventured. "Is that what I hear you saying?"

"That's really churchy language, I know, but I guess you could say there was a new dynamic between me and God. A new connection."

"This is the part where you ask me if *I* want to reconnect with God…"

"Well, do you?"

"I don't know, Maggs. I feel like it would be really hypocritical to just say, 'Hey God, it's me, Kyla, the one who pushed you away and didn't want anything to do with you.'"

"God has some broad shoulders. It wouldn't bother him a bit."

"Here's what I'll promise you, Maggs. I won't give you a categorical no, but I need some time to process everything. Are you good with that?"

"Absolutely. I'm sorry if I sounded preachy."

"You didn't—and I was the one who asked in the first place."

SCOTTY

Dogs have a ridiculously keen sense of smell. I remember one time when Kyla had friends over. She kept raising her voice at me when I sniffed the cuffs of the pants they were wearing. I got the sense she wanted me to stop, but you might as well tell the ocean to stop sending waves to the shore. Those pants were like a smorgasbord of scents. I could tell where these people had been. Often they had gone to Wascana Park. I could smell it. Or they might have walked through a back alley. I couldn't *not* take a sniff. I guess I'm too curious, but I've always loved to absorb the scents of the neighbourhood.

All this is to say that as the afternoon faded to evening, the scents from the two-legs around us became a bit much, even for me. There was the sickly sweet smell from a lady who had liberally showered herself in cheap perfume that morning. Piled onto that was the stale breath from a snoozer in the seat behind us.

The real kicker was the guy beside the lady, who wasn't the freshest-smelling chip in the bag. And we had nowhere to go.

We got some air when my caregiver moved the bar on the small window beside her. It didn't help much. I felt like we were stuck in the stinkiest kennel in the world and left there to die.

When the bus finally came to a stop and we were able to get out, I was ecstatic to breathe the outside air. It was dark as the lady carrying me stepped off and moved toward a place with lots of people, some small fires, and tantalizingly tasty scents.

Rescue Lady—that's how I started to think of her—sat on a wooden bench and began tapping on a little handheld machine. Kyla had one just like it. Anyway, Rescue Lady put the machine back into her bag and then pulled out a small leather receptacle that held some paper and shiny coins.

She picked me up from the ground and handed a man some of these papers and coins. He returned a minute later with a plate of hot, steaming, deliciously savoury food. I could smell ochre, peanut butter, cayenne peppers, chicken, and tomato sauce. I knew this was going to be eaten by the Rescue Lady, but I held out some hope that I might have a few nibbles when she was finished.

Sure enough, she put the plastic plate on the ground later and I absolutely devoured what was left on it, placing my front paw on the plate to keep it from slipping while I licked up these last tasty morsels.

By now it was entirely dark except for lights from the road. Night had pushed day aside, which wasn't a big problem for me. I could still see decently well in the dark. I never met a dog who couldn't get around in darkness.

I was surprised so many people were still out and about. In Regina, the streets were virtually empty on my night walks with Kyla. Often there'd only be a few other two-legs with their dogs. But here I saw dogs being yelled at and chased away from the fires and food. I thought it would only be a matter of time before Rescue

Lady got chased away too, because of me, but I did my best not to draw attention to myself. I lay quietly under the bench and tried not to think about the slight throbbing in my leg.

Rescue Lady kept pulling out that machine from her bag and tapping it. She seemed to be expecting something to happen. I could smell nervousness escaping from her pores.

Scotty, you've had a major adventure, I thought to myself. *You better get some sleep.*

And that's what I did.

Kyla

Kyla was happy not to be left alone in a hotel room. Somehow the waiting seemed less nerve-wracking with Maggie around. Being busy helped too.

After their supper together, Maggie and Kyla both had to fill out reports for their aid organizations. The laptop keys hummed as they filed the details of the conference. Kyla hated this part of her job but knew that her newfound passion for women-led micro-enterprises wouldn't be enough. The stakeholders in Canada would need to be brought onboard… and that would only happen if she were able to tell the conference's success stories and provide the supporting statistics.

Kyla was putting the finishing touches on her report when she heard her phone ping. The message was from Sandra: "Just passed Dassouri. Should be in Ouagadougou in an hour or less. See you at the station."

"Maggie, this is it!" Kyla hurriedly checked her bag to make sure she had her passport and wallet. "Can I leave my stuff here, Maggs?"

"Of course! I'll come downstairs to make sure you get a taxi."

Getting a taxi wasn't a problem. The taximen knew that lots of tubabs stayed at the hotel, and they rightly assumed these people weren't likely to take public transport. Pretty much any time of the day or night, their taxis waited outside the hotel.

Kyla chose a white sedan with a yellow taxi sign affixed to the roof.

"No bags?" the taximan asked in surprise.

"No bags. Just making a quick trip to the station."

"Gare Centrale?"

Kyla had assumed there was only one station in Ouagadougou and felt safe in that assumption. "Yes. Gare Centrale."

Unlike many drivers in Ouagadougou, this one was relatively quiet. He didn't ask who she was going to meet, who she worked with, or why she was in Burkina Faso.

"Did you hear about the attempted coup?" he asked instead.

Thankfully, Kyla had read the headlines that morning. "Yes. It sounds like it was put down pretty quickly."

"It was. Compaore is a good president. And he has the military on his side. As long as that's the case, coups are not going to succeed."

Kyla felt a little unsure about this information, but she didn't want to contradict her driver, who seemed friendly and astute. She liked the fact that he was dressed smartly, even donning a chauffeur's cap to complete the picture.

She decided to continue the conversation. "But the article I read said that one of his officers has been arrested on charges of treason?"

"Yes, that's standard procedure. Trust me, the president probably knew about this attempted coup before it reached the planning stages. But someone has to be arrested. That's West African justice for you."

In less than fifteen minutes, the driver pulled over to the curb.

"Well, here we are," he said. "That'll be two thousand francs please."

Kyla knew she was paying the "white" price, but she was too excited and tired to negotiate a lower fare. She handed the man two one-thousand-franc bills and an extra five hundred bill as a tip.

She walked toward the station, holding her bag across her chest to discourage any would-be thieves. The building was an old brick-and-mortar holdover from the late 1800s when France had been expanding her empire.

She looked in vain for a row of parked buses. Considering the time of night, she was surprised to see people still walking about. But the last of the street food vendors were packing up their wares and leaning their makeshift wooden tables against the walls.

"Excuse me," she asked one young man. "Is this Gare Centrale?"

"Yes it is, ma'am."

"Thank you."

"No problem, ma'am."

The young man was busy strapping a bag onto his bicycle carrier and checking the pressure of his back tire. Kyla wandered inside the near-empty building, all the way to the platform for the railway tracks. There, a lone man was sweeping debris left behind by the day's travellers.

Not a bus in sight.

Just then her phone rang. "Hello?"

"Hi Kyla. This is Sandra. Where are you?"

"I'm at the station. Where are you? I can't see you anywhere."

"There are two stations in Ouagadougou. One for trains and one for buses. Are you seeing any buses around you?"

"No, Sandra. I'm at the Gare Centrale."

"Okay, that explains it. I'm at the Gare de l'Est."

"Ah! I knew this didn't feel right. How is Scotty?"

"Oh, he's pretty perky," Sandra replied. "Just chillin' here under a table, but I feel like we're gonna soon wear out our welcome if I don't order some more food soon."

"So good to hear you made it!"

"Yeah, it's all good. Hey, listen, do you think you could catch a taxi? Tell him to take you to Gare de l'Est. I'm sitting at a table beside a big green bus that says *Express* on it. Right now it's pretty much in the middle of a pack of other buses."

"Sounds good," Kyla said. "I'll be there as soon as I can."

"We're not going anywhere. See you soon."

Kyla wasn't one to kick herself. Yes, she had made a rookie mistake, but she was pretty sure she wouldn't have a problem procuring a taxi, however late the hour. As her dad had always said, "Control what you can control and don't sweat the rest."

She returned to the spot where the taximan had dropped her off. Several green vehicles were parked in the square. A man with a Che Guevara T-shirt stood smoking beside his taxi. His trendy jeans and sneakers made him look as American as any taximan in New York or Chicago; she was pretty sure that was the look he was going for.

"Taxi?" he cried as he saw Kyla approach.

"Oui," Kyla answered.

"Ou tu vas?"

"Gare de l'Est."

"Okay, hop in," he said with a smile.

Kyla wondered how these guys knew she wasn't from France. They switched to English as soon as she opened her mouth.

Must be the accent, she thought. *And the fact that the taximen are usually keen to practice their English.*

She climbed in the back and pulled on her seatbelt.

"One thing about you *blancs*, you always use your seatbelts," the taximan commented.

"Habit, I guess," Kyla said. "So how far is the Gare de l'Est?"

"Oh, not too far. We'll be there in no time."

Kyla realized too late that she should have negotiated a price for the ride before climbing in, but she was glad to hear it wasn't too far. She would soon be holding Scotty. The thought warmed her as she sat back and looked out the window.

Why aren't all these people at home at this hour? she wondered as she gazed at the people million about.

A lady with a child strapped to her back balanced a load of wash on her head. Two young men walked arm in arm, laughing. The driver swerved to avoid a donkey cart; firewood bulged over the cart's sideboards, a frayed rope doing its best to hold the sticks and logs in place.

The city lights grew less frequent and Kyla wondered how much further they would need to drive to arrive at the Gare de l'Est. It didn't surprise her that it would be on the outskirts of the city… but when she glanced at her phone, she realized that nearly twenty minutes had elapsed.

"Are we almost there?" she asked.

"Just about. I'm trying to avoid the main roads. Some demonstrations tonight about the arrest of the coup leader. Il est innocent, d'apres moi."

Kyla was glad the taximan couldn't see her smirk.

They're always innocent, she thought. *Every person in jail says he's innocent.*

The streetlights were non-existent by this time and Kyla began to feel uneasy. She tried to push away thoughts of abduction for ransom. Those things happened on backroads in the northwest part of the country. She had heard about a nun who had been held by jihadists for three years before being released. But the nun had been scooped up in Yaombe, hundreds of kilometres from Ouagadougou.

"Shouldn't we be there by now?" Kyla asked, trying to sound as calm as she could.

"Don't worry. We'll be there in a few minutes," he said.

Kyla felt increasingly uncomfortable and gingerly tried the handle of the door. Good. It wasn't locked. Worst case, she could jump out when the car slowed down.

By now she was sure she was being taken hostage. It was no longer an irrational thought; it was a certainty. There hadn't been a single streetlamp or passing car for the last ten minutes.

Kyla scoped the landscape and noted the bramble trees and elephant grass beside the road. In the headlights, she noticed a slight dip and sharp curve in the road ahead.

This was her chance to escape. Grasping her bag, she prepared to jump and roll. She could feel the fear and adrenaline rise to the surface.

Sure enough, the car slowed.

Now, Kyla, she thought as she gripped the door handle.

Because the taximan was focused on slowing for the corner and avoiding the huge puddle in the middle of the path, he didn't see Kyla prepare to exit.

By the time he pulled the car over, Kyla had jumped out.

She could not have chosen a better spot to exit. When her body finally stopped rolling, she rose and ran toward the darkness of the trees along the side of the road.

As soon as she was safely within the shadows of the brush, she looked back in the direction of the car.

"Come back," she heard the driver yell. "Don't be scared!"

Yeah, right. As if she would think of going back now.

She stayed low to avoid being caught in the beam of light surveying the ground around her. So he had a flashlight. What else did he have?

Long after the flashlight beam had disappeared, and after she had heard the car engine toggle through its gears and gain speed, she took a few tentative steps toward the road. She could see the taxi's taillights heading back to Ouagadougou, but she knew the driver might simply be pretending to drive away. He could easily double back and capture her again.

Kyla brushed off the dirt from her trousers and noticed a scrape on her left shin to match the one on her elbow. She was heartened to find that nothing seemed to be broken. Walking wouldn't be a problem.

She moved cautiously in the same direction the car had gone. If he doubled back, she would dive into the woods again.

She looked in her bag to pull out her phone, intending to call Sandra and explain what had happened. Even if she wanted to call an emergency number, though, she didn't know what it would be in Burkina Faso. She was pretty sure 911 wouldn't cut it here.

And that's when it hit her: there was no phone. She remembered laying it down beside her on the seat. Had she really been so dense as to leave her phone behind?

She frantically ran her hands through her bag. Passport, lip chap, hotel card, even a novel she'd picked up in one of the airport stores, but definitely no phone.

Great! Was there any way this nightmare could get worse?

On the bright side, she had opted for a practical pair of shoes that morning in place of the dressier high heels. She could walk all the way back to the city if necessary.

What had Sandra said? It might be a good time to start praying.

"Oh God, it's so hopeless," she whispered. "I don't know what to do. Thank you for helping me get out of that car with only a few scrapes and bruises. But I have no phone, no way of knowing where I am, and no one to help me. Please, Lord God, please, please help me."

Halfway through her prayer, Kyla heard a vehicle approach from behind her. Her first instinct was to run for the bushes, but something held her in place, almost as though her feet were stuck.

Above the gentle cadence of the engine, she heard a beating sound, along with voices. She repressed an urge to pinch herself because these sounds were all too familiar. How many times had she listened to the beat of a goat-skin drum in church and listened to the youth choirs belt out a chorus of praise to God?

As the vehicle got closer, she heard young voices singing praise songs. This was no car stereo. It had to be a travelling youth choir.

By now she could make out the shape of a small pick-up truck with many passengers riding in the back, as they were singing as they travelled.

She was soon bathed in the truck's headlights, still feeling unsure about how this was going to play out. Everyone, even people in remote Africa, perhaps especially in remote regions of Africa, knew better than to pick up a stranger for any reason.

But against all odds, the truck seemed to slow down. The singing had stopped and a young man leaned out the window.

"C'est qui?" he yelled.

"I need help!" she called back, then remembered to switch to French. "J'ai besoin d'aide!"

Either because she looked harmless or because the man detected her North American accent, the truck slid over to the side and came to a stop.

"What are you doing out here?" The young driver stepped out of the truck and approached with caution.

"I was in a taxi and I jumped out when I thought I was in danger. He was supposed to take me to the Gare de l'Est."

"Well, you were right to jump out. This is a long way from the gare. Jump in. We're going right by there. We'll drop you off. Are you okay?"

Kyla imagined that he was wondering about the abrasions on her arms and legs. "I'm all right. Got some cuts and bruises when I jumped out of the taxi, but I'll be fine."

As she climbed into the cab of the truck and sat next to the driver, she turned around and surveyed the youth in the back. They all wore expressions of genuine concern.

She felt safe with these people.

The man started driving again. "Why the gare at this time of night?"

"I'm meeting someone there. Long story, but I'm pretty sure my friend will be worried sick that I didn't show up."

"Just text them."

"I would, but my phone got left in the taxi."

"You can use mine." The young man handed her his phone.

"Thanks, uh…"

"Paul," he filled in. "You've had some rotten luck. What's your name?"

"Kyla. And yes, I guess I've had better days."

"But you're alive. That's something."

"Yeah, that's something for sure. Thanks so much for stopping."

"Let me ask you something, Kyla: are you a Christian?"

"Funny you should ask that," Kyla began, feeling somehow unsurprised by this new line of inquiry. "I haven't been what you would call a practicing Christian… but just before you showed up, I cried out to God for help."

"Isn't that just like God? You know, it's interesting. Before we left our village, an older Christian man told us, 'Be alive to the opportunities out there. You never know when you can make a difference in someone's life.' And then we come upon you at the side of the road. I tell you, that's God stuff!"

In spite of herself, Kyla laughed out loud. "Well, God stuff or not, I'm sure glad you came along when you did."

"Trust me," Paul said with conviction, "it was some serious God stuff! I'm no prophet, Kyla, but if you believe things happen for a reason, you might want to think seriously about what God is up to here. Maybe he's trying to get your attention."

Looking out the windshield, she saw that they had arrived at a station with buses clustered all around it like ships in a harbour. This must be the Gare de l'Est.

"Do you know where your friend said she'd be?" Paul asked.

"Just that she'd be next to a green bus with the word *Express* on it.

"There it is." He pointed to a bus directly in front of them. "I'll let you out here. If I get any closer, I won't be able to turn myself around. But I'll wait until you find your friend."

Kyla shuffled herself down the bench seat and opened the door. "Thank you ever so much, Paul. You can't know how much this means to me."

"You're welcome, Kyla. And think about what I said about God stuff. I don't think he's finished with you yet."

"I'm sure he's not. Thank you again."

Kyla saw the bus straight ahead and began to walk toward it, limping slightly and favouring her left knee.

SCOTTY

When I awoke, I noticed that a deep darkness had settled over the land. To be honest, this came as a relief for two reasons. First, the temperature had dropped and I felt like I could breathe easily once again. My nostrils didn't feel singed every time I took a breath. Second, my eyes weren't sore anymore. I know Police and his buds were used to the intense sunshine, but my eyes were burning up! I no longer felt like I needed to run to the shade of a tree.

Rescue Lady put down a plastic dish of water at the foot of the table where we rested. I was only too glad to lap it up. She was still staring at that machine in her hand, tapping vigorously. Whatever it was, she seemed to be entirely focused on it right now. Her eyes were doing that thing two-legs so often did when the hair above their eyes seemed to drop. She seemed very… *intense*, as if something were really bothering her.

At one point in the night, a mangy-looking mutt stared at me, lowering its head, then raised it again. I decided to be proactive.

"What are you lookin' at?" I growled.

Rescue Lady seemed surprised at my response to the dog and said something I can only assume was meant to express some chagrin. But she didn't understand how dogs relate to each other.

Sometimes it was best to let my fellow four-legs know where things were at.

Fortunately, the brown mutt decided to move along. I lowered my head between my front paws again, trying to look uninterested.

Two-legs could often obsess over time and that's what Rescue Lady seemed to be doing now. She struck me as disturbed. I wished she could have just relaxed, but that didn't seem to be in the cards tonight.

She looked down at me and spoke in a slightly calmer voice than she had used before.

That's when it happened. A lady stepped out of a moving vehicle with a bunch of people on the back of it, and whoever it was walking toward us.

I blinked a few times to make sure, but then I recognized her. It was Kyla! I barked loudly, straining at the rope around my neck. I was so happy that I just about toppled the table over.

Rescue Lady must have seen what was happening because she immediately unfastened the other end of the rope, which had been tied to the table. I ran as best I could with my gimpy leg, bounding toward Kyla.

She had seen me.

She swooped me up in her arms and stroked my back. Something wet was coming from her eyes and I knew that this happened sometimes with two-legs when they were either extremely happy or sad.

For my part, I licked her face, which got her laughing. The salt from her face tasted so good!

Throughout this time, Rescue Lady stood patiently off to the side. If she was annoyed at being left out, she didn't show it.

Finally, Kyla put me on the ground and gave a long hug to the lady who had brought me on the bus. They exchanged some words, and at one point Rescue Lady looked Kyla up and down and seemed to express surprise. I noticed some cuts and bruises on Kyla that hadn't been there when we'd left home all those days ago. Something unexpected had no doubt happened, but the important part was that we were together again, and I knew with certainty that I wasn't going to let her out of my sight again.

Kyla

Most of Kyla's friends described her as even-keeled, even nonplussed, but tears came unbidden and with force upon seeing Sandra and Scotty. Being an animal lover, Sandra seemed to understand the importance of letting Kyla and Scotty have their moment. She smiled to see Scotty so visibly excited at the sight of his owner.

"Someone is happy to see you!" Sandra commented after the licking and kissing had abated somewhat.

"Sorry." Kyla opened her arms for a hug. "I'm Kyla."

"Hi Kyla. I'm Sandra, but you probably had that figured out already."

Kyla smiled. "Yeah. That's true. Oh, Sandra, you wouldn't believe the night I've had!"

"I gathered that something had happened. I've been trying to phone you for the last three hours. You're all cut up."

"I asked the taximan to bring me here, but instead he started driving me to God knows where. It didn't feel right, so when the opportunity came I jumped out of his taxi and ran for my life. Also, I lost my phone. I'm pretty sure I left it in the cab."

"Oh, Kyla, that's crazy!" Sandra both looked and sounded alarmed. "Are the cuts from jumping out of the car then?"

"I rolled on some gravel and got a pretty good road rash."

"So how did you get here? You couldn't have walked all that way."

"That's the incredible part..." Kyla shook her head. "I kept to the shadows—you know, kind of walking back toward Ouaga—when I heard this vehicle approaching. I thought I heard singing coming from the back of the truck, so I decided to take a risk. It turned out to be a church youth group coming back from a meeting. They gave me a ride here. It was almost like they were expecting me."

"That's wild!" Sandra commented. "Sounds like God had your back."

"That's exactly what the driver said. And I did pray, Sandra. It might not have been pretty, but I did pray. That's when these guys showed up out of nowhere."

"West African angels!"

"You got that right! Oh, I just can't believe that Scotty's here. But look at his leg!"

"It doesn't look great," Sandra admitted. "But he's not one to complain. He was a real trooper."

"What do you think I should do about my phone?" Kyla asked.

Sandra pulled her phone from her own pocket. "Well, for starters, we should probably call your credit card company. Let them know what happened. Just in case that driver tries hacking into your phone. What kind of card do you have?"

"Visa."

"Good. Same as me." Sandra had already pulled her card out of her wallet and was dialling the number on the back of it.

In less time than Kyla would have imagined, she had sorted out the cancellation of her credit card along with putting a block on her phone number. One less thing to worry about.

"So how familiar are you with Ouagadougou?" Kyla asked.

"Not at all. I've only been here once, and it was for a conference a few years ago. We only stayed for a few days."

"You're coming with me then. I'm staying with a friend and I'm sure there'll be room for you too."

"Are you certain? I can just get a place nearby."

"Let you stay by yourself after all you've done for me?" Kyla smiled and shook her head. "I don't think so!"

Sandra and Kyla began to walk toward a row of green taxis waiting beside the road. Kyla held Scotty close to her chest, trying to avoid squeezing his front paw and leg.

"Sandra, I'm gonna let you pick the taxi. I haven't had the best luck with taxi drivers lately."

"Not a problem. I wouldn't feel like getting in another taxi either if I were you." Sandra approached a large man smoking beside his taxi. "Can you take us downtown?"

"Not if the dog is going too."

"Are you serious?" Sandra said indignantly. "Is that some kind of company policy?"

"That's *my* policy. Me and dogs don't get along."

"But look at him!" Sandra said. "He's just little."

"Look." The man flicked his cigarette into the street. "I had a bad experience once. Dogs don't come into this car."

By this time, Kyla was pulling Sandra away. The last thing she needed right now was a red-haired midwestern firecracker creating a scene.

They soon found a taxi man who was willing to take pets.

"Can you believe that guy?" Sandra said. "Did he think Scotty was going to attack him from the back seat?"

"I can believe just about anything. I mean, I'm in a car with an angel I've only just met, with an injured pet I haven't seen in days. On top of that, we seem to be on our way to our hotel rather than destinations unknown. I call that a win right now."

"You have a point there, Kyla. Who's your friend, by the way? The one you're staying with."

"Oh, she's an old school friend who works for US International Help. We're at the same conference."

"Cool! And what is this conference about?"

"How to encourage micro-enterprises in West Africa."

Sandra smiled widely. "Love it! There's some of that stuff starting to happen in Mali, but it's been slow."

The drive from the bus station to the hotel only took a few minutes. With the front desk clerk nearly asleep when they came through the lobby, no explanations were necessary.

Thankfully the clerk, looking up sleepily, didn't notice the dog being smuggled into the building, and Scotty kept quiet in Kyla's arms.

"Maggie!" Kyla whispered through the door when they got to the room. "It's me, Kyla. Open up."

Maggie appeared at the door in her pyjama shorts and T-shirt.

"Where have you been? I've been worried sick!" she said as she let Kyla, Scotty, and Sandra inside.

"Get ready for a long story, Maggs. If it hadn't happened to me, I wouldn't believe it myself…"

SCOTTY

Dogs live in the moment. We don't waste our time thinking about the future or about what might have been. In our dreams, we occasionally relive significant events from the day we've just experienced, but that's about as far as we reach into the past.

I'd say this tendency to live in the moment was an important factor in my reunion with Kyla. I don't know how we got separated, but I didn't have anything to do with finding one another after so many days of being apart. What I will say is that I've never been so happy to see a two-legs as I was this particular night. I was on the receiving end of a lot of affection and I didn't mind at all.

We got in a car, and after a while the vehicle came to a stop. Kyla stuffed me into a large handbag and spoke to me in a serious tone. I kept quiet and my head tucked down as we walked into a building.

Shortly after, she let me out. We were in a much smaller room with two beds and I gave a few yips of delight at being able to move about freely again.

But hearing the chiding tone of Kyla's voice, and seeing her finger pressed to her lips, I toned down the exuberance and fell silent.

Could a dog be happier than when it's with its owner, safe and sound in a cool, comfortable room? I doubt it.

After drinking from a large, elevated bowl with a tank, I settled down on the comfortable rug and listened to the companionable voices of Kyla and her two-legged friends.

Kyla

Owing to the lateness of the hour, Kyla provided an abbreviated version of the story to Maggie, who then suggested they double-check the airline regulations regarding small dogs in the cabin.

"Here it is," she said as she pulled up the information on her phone. "It looks like the airline will allow small dogs up to six kilos in the cabin as long as they're confined to a carry-on bag that has a waterproof lining."

"I definitely don't have one of those," Kyla admitted.

"Yeah, but this is West Africa. In the morning, we'll get a runner to go find one in the market," Maggie said.

"You really think we could find something like that here in Ouaga?"

Sandra shrugged. "I would guess you aren't the first person to need a bag like that. There's basically nothing that can't be found in an African market."

Sandra ended up sleeping on the small loveseat next to the television, snuggled into blankets from Maggie's bed. Lying in her own bed, Kyla's mind went round and round like a spinning top, the sound of the air conditioner eventually helping her fall asleep.

In the morning, Sandra took it upon herself to procure a carryon bag for Scotty while Kyla and Maggs confirmed travel details for Kyla's afternoon flight. No way would Kyla let the airline put Scotty in the hold of the airplane again—not if she had anything to say about it.

At around ten-thirty, Sandra came bounding into the room with a bag. "Found it!" she exclaimed.

"You didn't!" Kyla cried in disbelief.

"A piece of cake. Well, not quite a piece of cake, but never let it be said that these marketplaces in Africa don't have stuff. You just have to know how the system works."

Everything seemed to be falling into place—and then the phone rang.

"Who could that be?" Maggie wondered. She picked up the receiver and immediately handed it to Kyla.

"Hello?" Kyla answered.

"Is this Kyla Bouvier?"

Kyla thought she recognized the voice, but she couldn't quite place it at first. "Yes."

"This is Mungolo Traoré with the Bamako Airport Authority. How are you?"

"I'm fine, Mr. Traoré. And how are you?"

Kyla used to get exasperated at these perfunctory greetings, but she found them useful now; the extra time helped her settle her whirling mind.

"Fine, thank you," he said. "I couldn't get a hold of you with the number you left me, but I'm glad I was able to track you down."

"Yes, well, I'm afraid I had the misfortune of losing my phone, Mr. Traoré."

"Sorry to hear that, Ms. Bouvier. I just wanted to let you know that the airplane you're booked on has had some mechanical issues and the passengers have been asked to save hotel receipts for compensation from Air France. The next flight will be on Tuesday afternoon."

Kyla couldn't believe her ears. She didn't believe him. If she had to bet on it, she'd say Traoré was only buying time so his men could locate Scotty.

Just to be sure, she decided to ask the question. "And how is my dog, Mr. Traoré?"

"Oh, your dog is perfectly fine. I'm sure he'll be overjoyed to see you, but for the moment he is being well looked after."

That settled it for Kyla. She couldn't wait to get off the phone. "Well, thank you, Mr. Traoré. I guess I'll have to wait until Tuesday to be reunited with my dog. Take good care of him until then."

"Most certainly, Ms. Bouvier. We will. Have a good day."

Kyla sank into a chair and replaced the phone receiver with shaking hands.

"Well?" Sandra and Maggie asked simultaneously.

"That was the airport authority in Bamako. My flight has been delayed until Tuesday and Scotty is being taken good care of there."

Sandra let out a long sigh. "Didn't I tell you?"

"I'm so glad I listened to you. It's been nuts these last few days, but it was the right call. Nothing against Africa, but I can't wait to be back to boring old Regina," Kyla proclaimed. "Did my voice sound afraid?"

"Not at all. But didn't a tiny piece of you want to tell him to stick it, that your dog is right here beside you?" Maggie asked.

"A little, yeah, but I knew that would just complicate things even more. When in doubt, don't offer anything more than what you're being asked about."

"You sound like a character out of a John LeCarre novel," Maggie commented.

"John who?" Sandra asked.

Maggie turned to her. "John LeCarre. You know, *The Constant Gardener*."

"I don't go in much for gardening."

The other girls both laughed, then decided to go out and find something to eat. But someone had to stay with Scotty. Sandra volunteered to go downstairs and retrieve some breakfast food from the hotel lobby buffet.

She returned a few minutes later with baguettes, jam, coffee, tea, and cold cereal and laid it all out alongside some fresh mangoes and oranges.

"Wow, how did you manage that?" Kyla asked.

"I used to be a waitress in Omaha," Sandra explained. "Hitting the floor button with my elbow was the biggest challenge."

Scotty hadn't been forgotten, and soon a few tasty bits of baguette came flying his way. He seemed only too happy to wolf them down.

"I couldn't manage to carry up coffee, though," Sandra admitted.

"I'm on it!" Maggs said. "I know how Kyla takes hers. How about you, Sandra?"

"Just black, please."

"Be back in a minute."

After the hungry threesome had polished off their breakfast, Sandra raised a practical concern. "Shouldn't we try to get Scotty used to his little carrier?"

And that became the entertainment for the next hour.

SCOTTY

Have you ever been asked to get inside a bag only inches bigger than you are and then have a zipper close over you? That's what Kyla and her nutty friends were trying to make me do. They had to be kidding! I wasn't going in there of my own free will, I could tell you that.

They seemed insistent. Kyla used that urging kind of voice. Then she used that firm kind of voice…

Don't get me wrong. I'm not generally a disobedient dog. I like to keep things simple. I obey, I provide fun and entertainment, and my two-legs feeds me and gives me a place to hang out forever. It's really a pretty good gig.

But that little bag did not appeal to me in the least.

I'm pretty intuitive, and after seeing Kyla's distress I decided to give it a go. With her holding the side flap open, I crawled in and sat down. The space wasn't as small as I'd thought it would be. I lay down inside and found that I could easily move my head around. I had wondered about how I'd be able to breathe, but all kinds of air came in through the sides of this bag.

All three ladies started jumping up and down and clapping each other's hands. I don't know what I had done that so amazed them, but they seemed to be genuinely pleased with me for getting into the bag. Kyla even gave me a bone to chew on. Don't know where that came from! It was one of those bones that doesn't break and just feels so good on the gums and teeth.

After a bit, they let me out of the bag and I nestled up on Kyla's lap. Wow, did it feel good to be back with her. I wasn't going to let her out of my sight again, even if it meant climbing into a bag.

Kyla

As every post-9/11 traveller knows, even with tickets in hand, it pays to be at the airport a few hours early. With a departure of 15:00, the ladies decided that it would be best to begin packing. Maggie was flying out the following afternoon, so she helped Kyla get her things organized. Scotty slept contentedly at the foot of the bed while Kyla arranged her bags. She would only be allowed one carry-on, counting Scotty.

Sandra, bless her heart, had returned from her second trip to the market a little while ago, this time with a larger bag that would work as checked luggage.

"Sandra, you've been pretty quiet for the last hour," Maggie observed. "Anything the matter?"

"I'm fine," she responded unconvincingly.

Maggie raised an eyebrow. "As my favourite actor from *The Italian Job* would say, fine stands for 'freaked out, insecure, neurotic, and emotional.'"

"Well, that kind of hits it on the head. I mean, you two are going back to your lives in North America and I'm staying right here in the heat and sweat of West Africa. Not only that, but I'm pretty sure I'll have some questions to answer."

Kyla paused in her packing to consider this. "What kind of questions?"

"Well, you know, the whole unexpected trip to Burkina Faso. I didn't really have time to tell my boss what I was up to."

"How much contact do you have with your boss?" Kyla asked.

"I check in with him about twice a week. Being the weekend, he won't be texting until Monday... but if he wants me to come to the office in Bamako, I'm kind of hooped," Sandra explained. "He's really chill. I'm sure he would understand. He's also an animal lover, so I know he won't be mad. It's the other people I'm afraid of."

"What other people?" Maggie asked.

"The ones who were looking for Scotty. They'll be asking around. I didn't tell anyone I was taking Scotty to Burkina Faso, but I'm sure lots of people saw me with him. They'll want to know what I was doing with that dog and why I left in such a hurry."

"Wow," Kyla said. "I've been so worried about Scotty that I never thought about the risks *you* were taking, Sandra. I'm so sorry I put you in this predicament."

"You didn't put me in anything. As I recall, this whole thing was my idea."

Kyle smiled at her new friend. "And a brilliant one too!"

"Would you two pray for me?" Sandra asked. "I just need to know God's peace right now."

The request took both Kyla and Maggie by surprise.

"I will," Kyla offered. She noticed the look of surprise in Maggie's eyes. "Sandra could use some prayer. It might not sound too pretty, but I would be glad to pray for you."

She closed her eyes and began.

"Lord God, we are your children. We mess up so much, but you still love us and you care about us. See Sandra right here, Lord? She needs your help. She needs some wisdom. It's not like I haven't been there. I know exactly what she feels like right now. So we're asking you to do something big. We're asking you to give her a huge helping of your peace right now. Help her do the exact things she knows she should do. Be her peace right now, God. Amen."

When Kyla opened her eyes again, she saw that Sandra's aspect and demeanour had shifted considerably. No longer agitated or afraid, she brought herself forward on the loveseat.

"That's it! Thank you so much, Kyla." Sandra threw her arms around Kyla and gave her a big midwestern hug. "I know exactly what I have to do!"

"Well, that's good. And what is that, Sandra?"

"I'll just tell the truth, that's all."

Kyla laughed. "The truth is always refreshing."

"I mean, think about it. They're going to ask why I took Scotty to Burkina Faso, because they'll be able to track my ticket purchase. I'll just tell them about how I saw Scotty's information on Facebook and connected with you. Again, social media is traceable. They can see that I've been in touch with you. So in this case, the truth is key. I don't have to rehearse a series of lies. It's all on public record."

"Including that part about our mistrust of the system," Kyla reminded Sandra.

"Yeah, but that part was on the phone, which you don't happen to have anymore."

"But you do, Sandra."

"Not for long. My minutes were about to run out and I've had some issues with the network lately. I'll 'lose' my SIM card, buy a new one here in the market, and switch servers. Easy-peezy. They can check my phone, but they won't find anything on it. I'll just stick to the Facebook angle. As long as you don't make any noise from your end in Canada, I think this whole thing will just go away, don't you?"

"Mr. Traoré will be more than happy to put this whole saga behind him," Kyla agreed. "I don't think anyone's going to lose their job over a lost dog, especially if a few weeks go by and he hasn't heard any complaints from me."

Kyla was right, of course. The director of the Bamako International Airport Authority would certainly have bigger issues to deal with than a lost dog. A hundred other files must be crying out for his attention. Kyla just needed to keep quiet, at least she hoped.

"Thanks for praying, Kyla. I feel at peace about this whole Scotty affair."

"You're welcome, Sandra. You are a hero in my books."

"Nothing heroic about what I did. Anyone who loves dogs would have done the same thing."

"Well, I hate to bust up this lovefest, but if you're gonna make that plane to Abidjan, we better get the show on the road," Maggie pointed out.

"All right, Scotty." Kyla pointed to the doggie carryon. "Time to rock and roll."

SCOTTY

The next few days were like a tranquil pond on a late summer evening. Did I love being cooped up in a bag for eighteen hours? Absolutely not. But the fact that Kyla was right beside me the whole way made the trip bearable. Dogs tend to take their emotional cues from their owners, and I have to tell you: Kyla was calm and cool the whole time.

After sitting a long time in a waiting area, I heard a man call out loudly enough that his voice seemed to bounce off the walls.

Kyla coaxed me into that crazy little bag she had with her and carried me to an area where lots of people were finding their seats and stuffing bags above their heads.

I'll spare you the details of the next day and a half other than to tell you that I was content to sit at Kyla's feet in that bag as opposed to waiting in a lonely room with eardrum-shattering noise.

You know that old expression, "There's no place like home"? Well, there really is no place like home. I could have kissed the carpet when I walked into Kyla's place in Regina. She seemed to think it amusing when I catapulted around the house like a crazy dog, even on my bum leg. I hobbled through the kitchen, my claws clicking along the lino, through the hallway to Kyla's room, over to the TV room, into her study, and then back to the cozy kitchen again. If dogs could sigh, that's what I would have done as I lay down next to the heat register.

Resting my head between my front paws, I thought of all the crazy things that had happened to me. My leg felt a lot better. Every so often, though, I thought back to that moment when the stick crashed into my leg. It reminds me not to run so recklessly.

I can't help wondering about the kind of "normal" life most dogs have where Police comes from. Brutal. Where I live, a kid throwing a stick at a dog with intent to injure would elicit a sharp rebuke.

I often reflect on my time with Police. Why was he so kind to me? Why did he go out of his way to help? I must have seemed like a strange creature, barely a member of the same species. The only explanation I can come up with is that he was treated with some measure of kindness by his own two-legs, who gave him at least one square meal a day. They didn't hit him, and they expected him to bark when strangers were nearby.

I think dogs take on the characteristics of their owners, whereas some traits are inbred. I really believe that. For example, I was born to dig. That's just what I do. Kyla has the carpet to prove it! And I can't see a squirrel without giving chase. I just can't. Kyla has to keep the leash extra short and taut when she knows we'll be walking close to those pesky little guys.

But I learned kindness from Kyla.

So maybe Police was kind to me because his owners were kind to him. That has to be why he was so good to me.

I often wonder how he is. Is he still hanging out with Nicky and the others? Is he healthy? Is he still chasing after those female four-legs when nature beckons?

My life changed after meeting Police. I don't whine nearly as much. I appreciate what I have. I mean, I *really* appreciate what I have. Life is good for me. I only hope that in some small way, or even a big way, Police will be repaid for his kindness.

Police, wherever you are, good night.

Epilogue

The return trip is a lot less eventful than Scotty makes it sound. In Abidjan, Kyla is made to pay a "holding tax," supposedly for the inconvenience of having a pet in the waiting area of the airport between flights. This unexpected cost is never satisfactorily explained to her. Seeing no other way, though, she agrees to pay the ten thousand francs.

The layover in Paris is six hours long, during which Scotty urinates on a stanchion in the Charles de Gaule airport. Kyla manages to tidy up the mess with the help of a sympathetic cleaning lady who just happens to be mopping floors nearby. That is after Scotty, on the shuttle ride to Terminal B, growls at a man wearing chains and bits of metal on his clothes and body.

As for Maggie, she arrives home to Washington, or Crazy Town, as she likes to refer to it. Apart from a brief discussion with her boss about her charges for room service in Ouagadougou—"I was hungry. What can I say?"—she settles back into her work routine like an exhausted infant snuggling into her crib. She finds her work exhilarating and can't imagine not drawing up proposals for aid money to flow a little more responsibly into sub-Saharan Africa.

She keeps in touch with Kyla through the usual social media channels and the two friends enjoy biweekly chats on Friday nights when neither of them is doing much. Their adventure in Ouagadougou becomes fodder for laughs, reflection, and philosophical discussions about how only God could have pulled it off. Both agree on that point.

When Sandra returns to Sanankoroba, nothing comes of her trip to Ouagadougou, just as she predicted. Her boss concludes their discussion of the event with a warning: "Next time you decide to make a major trip like that, I better know about it. And you better have heard me say, 'No problem. See you when you get back.'"

The local police, at the behest of the Bamako Airport Authority, question her about what happened to the dog. She explains that she saw a message on Facebook about a lost dog, then contacted the owner and agreed to bring him to Ouagadougou. The police say they will check Facebook to confirm her story, which Sandra knew would happen. She doesn't expect to hear from them again, though, and she doesn't. The case is closed.

No doubt Mr. Traoré of the airport authority is only too happy to turn the page on what could have been an extremely embarrassing situation for him.

For all the dog owners out there, look over at that canine species lying contentedly next to you—and breathe. Thank the Lord that you have a member of the family who is more loyal and loving than many humans will ever be. You're likely sharing life with a Scotty. But don't forget about all the dogs like Police out there.